1-800-CUPID

A Sweet Contemporary Romance Novella

JOSIE RIVIERA

This book is dedicated to all my wonderful readers who have supported me every inch of the way.
THANK YOU!

CHAPTER ONE

*T*wenty thousand dollars.
Click.

Candee Contando licked her dry lips. She'd done it. She'd placed an online bid on a home-auction website for the Victorian mansion on Thompson Lane. Her dream home, her dollhouse. Her dilapidated project.

Two years of savings. Gone.

No matter. Under her guidance, she'd transform the mansion to its former majestic state, painted a mustard-yellow offset by ornamental burnt-sienna "gingerbread" trim. The sounds of children's giggling and music and barking beagles—yes, beagles—would echo across all five acres of the property.

She surveyed her offer and beamed, savoring the moment.

Now if she only could ensure that no one else bid on the property and drove up the price.

She studied the ticking clock on the website. Stay optimistic, she told herself. Deteriorated by age and wear, the Victorian would scare off any prospective buyer.

She pushed away from her desk and surveyed her real

estate office. Although only one room, she prided herself on the cheery décor. One wall featured photos of North Carolina —the majestic peaks of the Blue Ridge parkway and scenic waterfalls. Below the photos hung a map of the area with local real estate listings highlighted by pushpins.

She peered out the window into the street below. Since noon, a bright sun had been at odds with January's wind—a wind crazy in its intent to blow the streetlights off their wires.

For the umpteenth time, she checked her nonringing cell phone for messages. Surely the real estate market in Roses, North Carolina, would improve. Didn't prospective home buyers begin looking in January? And wouldn't these buyers call her rather than her competitors? Candee prided herself on her professionalism and up-to-date listings.

Then why hadn't she made a single sale since August?

On the heel of that depressing assessment came a cheerful one. In two hours, she and her older sister, Desiree, planned to enjoy dinner at Desiree's country club.

Candee stepped back to her desk and switched off the computer.

Two single women in their late twenties, she mused, spending Friday night alone and dateless, four weeks before Valentine's Day.

Her cell phone rang, most likely Desiree firming up dinner plans and reminding Candee not to be late. Regardless of what time Candee met her older sister anywhere, Desiree always arrived before her.

Candee clicked on her phone. "1-800-Cupid," she said with a laugh.

"Contando Realty?" a man asked.

"Yes, yes ..." So much for professionalism. Candee felt her cheeks color. She hurried to her desk, dropping into the chair and switching her phone to speaker. "Are you looking to buy a home today, sir?"

"I am." The man hesitated. "Is this the correct number?"

She powered on her computer. "Absolutely."

"I'm new to the area and checked into the Roses Hotel last night," he said.

Envisioning the rundown hotel, Candy raised her eyebrows. Although in all fairness, the hotel was the only lodging open in the winter. Roses, North Carolina, was a summer tourist town known for bubbling hot springs and cool mountain temperatures.

Her fingers poised on the keyboard. "I'm more than happy to assist. Your name?"

"Teddy. Teddy Winchester." He had a deep voice, a slight southern drawl.

"What type of home are you searching for, Mr. Winchester?"

"The worst home in the best neighborhood."

Yup. It figured. No significant sales commission to pay the mort-gage this month. Fortunately, her part-time job at the local hardware store was stable, although the pay was meager.

She scrolled through the listings. "For yourself, sir?"

"I'm an investor."

"How many bedrooms and baths?"

"Three bedrooms, two baths. Single family and one level."

"Budget?"

"Anything below $50,000."

She rubbed the back of her neck. *Who did he think she was, a miracle worker?*

"Mr. Winchester, the nicer neighborhoods in Roses are priced well above $100,000."

"Nope. Too high."

Certainly a man of few words.

"Perhaps—"

"I'll take another look on the Internet." He seemed to ignore her completely. "Thanks anyway."

She wouldn't lose a potential sale.

"Wait." She feigned checking a non-existent schedule. "I may have an opening this afternoon. I know the area well and I'll find properties to show you. Will three o'clock work?"

"In a half hour? Fine. I admire a realtor who works fast. Should I meet you at your office? The address is listed on the Internet."

Candee verified the street number and ended the phone call with a cheery, "See you at three."

She clicked off and checked her watch. Thirty minutes wasn't enough time to drive to her apartment and change. Her worn jeans and blue flannel shirt would have to suffice.

Immediately, she phoned Desiree. "I may be late for dinner."

"I'm so glad it's you," Desiree said. "Scott, a new lawyer at the firm, asked me out tonight. Barring the fact the invitation was last minute, I said yes. Desperation, right?" She paused. "Can we plan for dinner together tomorrow night instead?"

"Right, sure. The reason I called is because I have a client who's interested in seeing some properties."

"You have a real live client?" Desiree cut immediately to the question.

Candee envisioned her sister, thick blonde hair piled high, sitting behind a mahogany desk in her law firm. Proper, composed, every inch the high-powered attorney. Desiree had proven that, with the right help, a disadvantaged childhood could lead to a successful adulthood. She worked late hours at her law firm advocating justice for low-income families and their children.

"He's an investor," Candee said.

"Maybe he's tall, dark, and handsome?" Desiree said with deceptive casualness. "And rich?"

"Investors are usually short bald men." Candee adjusted her shirt's wrinkled collar, then checked out the frayed hem of her jeans. She let out a frustrated groan and ran a hand through her unruly auburn waves.

"You'll need a rich man if you plan to go through with your insane idea to purchase that Victorian," Desiree said. "The place will eat up all the money you hope to earn in a lifetime."

"I'll handle most of the work myself. Remember, when we lived in foster care, I learned carpentry from the family who took us in."

"How will you offer a quality after-school environment to disadvantaged kids if you're busy driving nails into crumbling walls?"

"Watch me." Briefly, Candee squeezed her eyes shut. It was her turn to pay it forward.

"Well, don't discount short men. They prefer tall, willowy red-heads with green eyes," Desiree said. "Who knows? He might be struck by Cupid's golden arrow when he meets you. This guy might be the one."

Candee drew in a breath. "The one what, exactly?"

"Your partner, your love, your support system. The one who can help pay off the mountainous amount of debt you'll incur if you actually buy the biggest dilapidated disaster in the state."

"Someone supportive? For me? After what happened?"

Desiree's voice grew quieter. "Not every guy pretends to be something he's not."

A lump lodged in Candee's throat. No man was worth having her heart broken again, although she didn't vocalize her feelings. Desiree was an eternal romantic.

With a promise to meet her sister on Saturday evening, Candee clicked off and bent to pick up a broken pencil lying on the floor.

Two years since he'd walked out, and she still felt it, not in tears, but in the careful way she kept people at a certain distance. Some lessons didn't fade. They just changed shape. Her ex had taught her the hardest. She wasn't interesting enough, pretty enough, or vivacious enough.

While she confirmed two house showings for Mr. Winchester, she pulled on her cream-colored woolen jacket and wound an emerald-green paisley scarf around her neck. A quick glance in the mirror — pinched cheeks, a touch of rose lip balm, auburn curls gathered into a ponytail — and she pushed open the exit doors and stepped outside.

The sun had buried itself under a formless cloud, and a swirl of wind blew her scarf across her face. She tucked it securely beneath the collar of her jacket.

The day was typical January weather for Roses, undecided if it was warm or cold.

CHAPTER TWO

Teddy Winchester pondered for the umpteenth time how he'd ended up in Roses, North Carolina. Certainly the town was charming, tucked along a backdrop of the Blue Ridge Mountains. He'd taken a ride around the region before he'd checked into the hotel. The shopping seemed adequate and the town center exuded storybook appeal, retaining a New England quaintness, complete with a bandstand.

Rob, his not-so-silent business partner in Florida, had assured Teddy the North Carolina weather was always cooperative, even pleasant for mid-January. And the area teemed with real estate bargains because Roses, population five thousand, had never fully recovered from the recession.

Rob was wrong on both counts. Relentless gusts battering under the drafty hotel's window had sent a chill through Teddy all morning while he'd sat in his room, and the inventory of low-priced homes on real-estate websites proved nonexistent.

Roses wasn't what he'd hoped for. He needed a quick turnaround investment to help pay for his nephew Joseph's physical therapy. A horrific car accident and the loss of his nephew's father had left Joseph traumatized and weak, and the extensive physical therapy included strength building and stretching.

Teddy took a deep breath, still reeling from his older brother's death. *Christian, we promised to never desert each other. And now you're gone.*

In an effort to keep busy, Teddy perused his email, then texted an abridged list of instructions to his secretary on how to proceed with the sale of his late brother's farm. He assumed Christian retained life insurance, which would help pay for the mountain of medical bills steadily piling up, as well as lawyers' fees. The papers declaring that Teddy was Joseph's legal guardian weren't finalized yet. The courts took their time, although the will guided the court's decision.

With a sigh, he tapped in Rob's business number.

Rob's gruff voice answered on the fifth ring. "Rob's Marvelous Muffins."

"Hi Rob. Is Joseph around?" Teddy asked.

"He's up to his elbows in Valentine muffin ingredients. A four-year-old's favorite activity is making a mess with a cupful of flour, right?" Rob chuckled. "I'll put him on speaker."

"Hi Uncle Teddy!" Joseph's high-pitched voice vibrated through the phone. "Mr. Rob and I are putting a surprise in our muffins and writing something special on each one. Wanna know what's inside?"

Teddy laughed. "Then it wouldn't be a surprise, right?"

The boy hesitated. "Right."

"Is there anything we can do about that?"

"I can save a muffin for you, Uncle Teddy."

"Great idea, buddy. I'll fly to Miami in a couple weeks, and we'll eat muffins together at Mr. Rob's bakery. Okay?"

Joseph giggled. "Okay."

It was the first time he'd heard the boy laugh since his father had died.

"I love you, Joseph," he said softly.

"Love you too, Uncle Teddy."

Rob got back on the phone. "He's a good kid. You should see how he's mixing the butter and sugar together."

"Maybe he's a born baker like you, Rob."

"Or a farmer like you."

"I was never good at farming." Which was true. It wasn't until he'd met Rob and gone into real estate that he'd discovered his forte.

"Maybe you haven't discovered the right crop. Try tomatoes. Those plants grow regardless of—Hang on a sec." Rob turned away from the phone, but Teddy could still hear him directing one of his employees to be careful attaching the food grinder to the heavy-duty electric mixer he'd recently purchased. His voice returned to normal strength as he inquired how the house hunting was going.

"I'm meeting a local realtor this afternoon."

"Shouldn't take long. It's a buyer's market." He barked another order to one of his employees, then goaded, "You miss slaving over a hot oven?"

Teddy could easily visualize the twinkle in Rob's crystal-blue eyes. "I haven't baked so much as a boxed cake in years," he said, chuckling.

He and Rob had met years earlier at a cooking class for men. Teddy had soon discovered his speciality would never include burning another muffin, but Rob had gone on to build a successful chain of bakeries in the greater Miami area. Teddy could practically inhale the delectable, sugary aromas coming from Rob's spotless commercial kitchen.

"And I'll take Joseph to his equestrian session this weekend," Rob was saying. "The kid has really formed a connection with horses."

"Exactly the reason his therapist advised it," Teddy replied. "She said horseback riding would reduce Joseph's anxiety after the trauma of the accident."

"She's right," Rob said. "And she's such a pretty thing, isn't she?"

"Rob, she's Joseph's therapist."

"Yeah, yeah, I know. And she's a few years younger than me, anyway." Rob gave an exaggerated whistle. "Remember to keep me in the real estate loop."

"Do I have a choice?" Teddy grinned. He was impatient with lawyers and their endless legal jargon and talk of probate court. However, with the man and mentor he owed his real-estate start-up business to, Teddy's patience was limitless.

"Hey, thanks for watching Joseph for me," he added.

"What are oddball friends for? Your job is to snag the best buy in Roses." The usually brash Rob tempered his tone. "And Joseph's no bother, you know. When someone's down and out they need help, right?"

"These past few months ... Thank you. For everything." Teddy clicked off and stared at the phone. Sometimes, he didn't know what he would've done if Rob hadn't been there to pick up the pieces after Christian's death.

He checked his watch, then pulled on a gray T-shirt. He was still half-wet from his shower and the T-shirt stuck to his body. He shook his damp hair, threw on a Florida State base-ball cap, stuck his wallet in his jeans pocket, and zipped up an olive-green vest. Out in the parking lot, he fired up the engine of his red truck, and at exactly three o'clock arrived at Candee Contando Realty. He needed someone experienced to help him get just the right property, and from the Internet reviews he'd read, Mrs. Contando had been in business over thirty years.

He walked to the entrance of an older brick building housing various offices and stopped midstep, admiring the beautiful young woman waiting in the doorway. The collar of a cream-colored jacket framed her oval face, along with an absurdly colorful green scarf. A pair of tiny gold cross earrings dangled from her ears. Her features were all high cheekbones and generous lips.

He tipped his baseball hat. "Hello. I'm supposed to meet Mrs. Contando here."

"I'm *Miss* Contando, although please call me Candee." Her smile enhanced her fascinating emerald eyes.

His heartbeat slowed and he had to prompt himself to swallow. "This is *your* realty?"

"Actually, it was said to be my mother's company for a while." She pushed back a stray wisp of auburn hair, handed him a business card, and then extended her hand. "Are you Mr. Winchester?"

"Teddy." Tight jeans emphasized her shapely legs and rounded hips. This woman's stunning good looks could stop traffic.

"I expected someone older," he managed to say.

She let go of his hand, swept her gaze up his six-foot frame, and grinned. "I expected someone shorter."

He met her grin, debating where he should look next.

Her lovely face enhanced by a sprinkle of freckles? Nope, not at all professional to stare. Instead, he gazed at the weathered door behind her and cleared his throat. "Did you find any listings?"

Her mouth curved into a polite smile. "Yes. Ready to see your future house?"

Unexpectedly, he felt drawn to her. She wasn't at all what he'd expected, although his good sense warned him away. He was completely satisfied with being single, having made peace with that reality ever since his one serious relationship with a woman had ended badly. He'd lost his self-reliance once, and once was enough.

He gestured toward his truck. "Should we use my vehicle or yours?"

"Mine." She pointed to a rusted Honda Civic. "I'll drive. I know these roads well."

He opened the car door for her, then came around and settled in the passenger seat.

She buckled her seatbelt. He buckled his, then took in a quick breath. A faint whiff of her scent lingered in the air. Roses. He grinned. Why not?

"So, Candee, have you lived in Roses all your life?"

She glanced at him. "I've lived here and there."

She returned her attention to the road, and an overlong moment passed in silence.

He waited for her to continue. When she didn't elaborate, he asked if he could turn on the radio. The station was set to Classic Rock and "Unchained Melody" by the Righteous Brothers came on, the heartfelt lyrics about "Oh, my love, my darling," filling the little car.

Teddy was about to suggest they try for more upbeat music when she gushed, "I love this song."

Okay, he thought. She must be a romantic.

"How many showings did you schedule?" he asked.

"Two, both in Glenhaven." Flicking on her signal, she turned onto another road. "You want three bedrooms and two baths, correct?"

"The perfect flip house."

"You don't intend to live in the property?"

"Nope. I want an easy fixer-upper that won't take longer than six weeks to renovate. I'm working with another investor, and we intend to make a quick and substantial profit."

"Don't we all," she murmured.

Their gazes met and they shared a grin.

Soon, they were driving past neatly manicured lawns and one-story homes.

She stopped in front of a beige bungalow, parking on the street. "The previous owners relocated, and this house has been on the market over sixty days." They got out and walked toward the house. As you can see—" she gestured to the tidy neighborhood and matching mailboxes—"Glenhaven is lovely."

"The neighborhood is too cookie cutter." He stood on the front porch and studied mismatched shingle patches nailed to the roof. "Needs some work."

"Inside, the home is beautifully decorated."

"The bigger the mess, the bigger the profit." Automatically, he provided the investor's mantra. "What's the asking price?"

"One hundred thousand dollars, although the owners are willing to negotiate."

He shook his head. "Too expensive." *Why did realtors try to sell homes over the buyer's stated limit?*

Noting Candee's downcast expression, he lightened his tone. "Are there any other homes in this town under fifty thousand?"

"There is ... one." She paused and pressed a finger to her lips, seeming to search for a reason not to answer.

He overlooked her lack of enthusiasm. "Price?"

"That particular house is listed on an internet auction site and meets none of your criteria." She paused. "It's a rambling Victorian and—"

"Where is this house?"

"On Thompson Lane at the edge of town. It's unoccupied."

"How much land comes with the property?"

"Five acres."

"Can the land be sold off in parcels? Is it zoned commercial or residential?"

"You can get on the website and download the report." She slid into the driver's seat and shut the door.

Had he heard a grunt of disapproval?

"Sorry I can't help you, Teddy," she continued, when he got into the passenger seat. "I'll drive you back to my office to get your truck, and I'll phone if anything in your price range becomes available."

Now he had to beg her to view a property? She might be gorgeous, but she was certainly the world's worst realtor.

"Do you have the lockbox code to this Victorian, Candee?"

She raised her delicate brows. "Yes, but—"

"I assume an appointment isn't necessary if no one lives there."

She inserted the key into the ignition. "My pleasure."

He didn't know why, although he'd bet she was being sarcastic.

A few minutes later she turned onto Thompson Lane. As they passed an elderly man with gray hair and glasses perched on his nose, she waved, explaining he was Mr. Dunworthy, a widower who owned a Queen-Anne-style home two doors away. He'd lived in the neighborhood forever and refused to give up his large home, although it was becoming more and more difficult for him to maintain.

She drove to the end of the road, sped up a circular driveway and parked in front of an imposing three-story house. An octagonal tower soared from the steep multigabled roof. Century-old trees flanked both sides of the property. On one corner of the overgrown front lawn, an oak tree boasted a tire swing. Teddy imagined himself pushing Joseph on that swing. Joseph needed to play more, needed fresh air. He'd been so pale since his father's death.

No, Teddy told himself. Quick and easy sale.

Of course, he could purchase the property for the land and build five new homes, more than tripling his profit. Or build low-income housing. Rob would agree with that decision.

He rounded the car to open the door for her, but she'd already gotten out. They stood side by side and stared at the house. For the first time in many years, he drank in the stillness of a cool winter afternoon, admiring a home he'd only imagined in his dreams—and was well aware of the insane impulse to hold Candee's hand as they walked to the front door.

He extended his hand to her.

She stared at him in surprise, but then she took his hand.

"The home is beautiful, isn't it?" she said as they walked to the front porch together.

It was, although the Victorian sat beneath layers of peeling yellow paint that marred its exterior and several of the windows were boarded up. A covered front porch curved around to the side, and there was also a side entrance. Teddy imagined white wooden rocking chairs, a row of lush Boston ferns, and ceiling fans spinning lazily on a warm summer afternoon.

The land, the land, he reminded himself.

Candee dropped her hand and tapped in the code for the lockbox. She tipped her head toward the purple front door. "In its former glory days, this home reflected the wealth of the owners—the Langrone family. They owned a prosperous knitting mill in Roses."

"And then?"

"And then the mill went out of business. Too much foreign competition. The Langrones declared bankruptcy and moved out shortly afterward. All the owners since then moved in with high expectations until they discovered they weren't able to maintain the upkeep."

What a waste of a beautiful home.

As if she'd read his thoughts she lingered on the porch, a wistfulness in her gaze. "This Victorian was built in 1889 and definitely requires TLC."

An absolute understatement, Teddy decided, when they walked in. The outside needed extensive work, and the hardwood floor of the grand foyer was badly gouged and scratched.

Candee flicked on a light switch. Nothing happened, and she offered an apologetic shrug. With lights not working, they were left in semidarkness. And although the odor in the entrance hall stopped him cold, she didn't miss a beat and continued walking.

"This is the kitchen," she was saying. "The cabinets are an olive color ..."

"What's left of them." He eyed the traditional arched raised panel doors and a lone cabinet left on the floor. So much beauty amidst so much neglect.

He stepped onto rusty linoleum. Luxury vinyl it was not because the floor felt soft and spongy beneath his work boots. Water damage, and hopefully not too extensive and requiring a floor joist.

Candee caught the focus of his gaze. "Avocado was a popular color in the 70's when the owners updated the kitchen."

"Avocado is back in style," he replied.

Hadn't Rob uttered the same words when he'd designed his showy corporate office in Miami?

Teddy opened and closed a cabinet door and examined the hinges. "With lots of elbow grease and white paint, these cabinets might work. Better than tossing them in a landfill."

Candee shook her head. "Nothing in this kitchen is

salvageable." She opened the oven door. With a shriek, she slammed it shut.

He inspected the grease-encrusted stove burners. "I'd install stainless steel appliances. The stove can stay. Six burners are a good selling feature, and the microwave can be mounted above the stove. Granite countertops, travertine flooring, a dishwasher, disposal ..." He swung around. "If I open this wall, there'd be an expansive view of the yard, which would be great for kids."

He didn't miss her speculative glance at his ring finger when he mentioned children.

"I'm not married," he said. "It's just me and my four-year-old nephew, Joseph."

She hesitated. "Where is he?"

"He's in Miami spending the next few weeks with my business partner, Rob. Rob's the one who got me started in real estate."

He'd said too much. How could he put into words the way his gut split every time he pondered Christian's death, or the pain Joseph had endured because of his numerous operations, or how Teddy had recently debated selling everything and starting over—somewhere quiet and peaceful—away from the high-pressure lifestyle of fast-paced Miami?

"Every home I take on, I treat as my own," he whispered.

Although this home wouldn't be here, because every bone in his practical body insisted it should be demolished.

He ran the faucet, and rusty water spewed into the chipped porcelain sink.

"City water and sewers," Candee said.

"Good. No septic issues or a dry well save money. What's this house going for?"

"No one knows the final price with an auction."

"Square footage?"

"Over 5500 square feet."

"This house is bigger than I thought." He pressed his lips together. "What's the current bid?"

She paused for a long while. "Twenty thousand dollars. You know you'll pour money into a house this size in order to get it back into shape."

"Did you know you're the exact opposite of a saleswoman, Candee?" With a grin, he stepped forward into what he presumed was the formal living room, appreciatively remarking on the marble fireplace with its updated gas fireplace and the twelve-foot ceilings.

"No use in traipsing through a ramshackle house—" Candee began.

"I noticed there's a dining room and parlor," he interrupted.

"Yes. And an adjacent library. And a music room."

That same wistfulness in her voice again.

He struggled to find the right words, debating whether to ask if she was upset about something. Hesitating, he changed direction. "Is the music room next?"

"You're the buyer." Had she silently inserted the adjective *foolish*?

He assessed the lengthening shadows signaling early nightfall. With no electricity, the house was growing darker by the minute.

As they headed into the music room, the toe of his boot caught on a torn piece of shag carpeting. He heard Candee call out a warning as he lost his footing and fell through the floor.

CHAPTER THREE

*C*andee peered through the hole in the floor into the shadowy basement. Although she heard Teddy's footsteps, she couldn't see him.

"Are you all right?" she called.

"Sure. I wanted to examine the basement, anyway. It appears to be a walk-out."

She leaned over, her eyes adjusting to the darkness. "What's it like down there?"

"I'll let you know in a minute." He switched on his cell phone's flashlight and peeked up at her, waggling his dark eyebrows. "Care to join me?"

He couldn't possibly be flirting.

"Uh no. I'll wait here, thanks."

Teddy pulled himself back up into the music room. "Maybe next time?"

With one hand in his worn jeans pocket, the other wielding a tape measure, he was rugged and impossibly good-looking, his muscled arms straining against a thin gray T shirt. He brushed dirt from his vest and yanked off his baseball cap. His wealth of black hair was mussed, and the late afternoon sun gilded thin strips of golden highlights to the tips. Perhaps he'd stepped right off the cover of the latest men's home improvement magazine without telling her.

Although she'd walked through this house many times, she hadn't ventured into the basement. Desiree often called Candee the opposite of a realist, although what would the world be like, Candee rationalized, without dreamers?

Teddy carried the broken kitchen cabinet from the kitchen and placed it over the hole in the floor.

As they continued through the house, he snapped photos with his cell phone.

"After I see the upstairs, I'll send these pictures to my partner Rob," he said.

She gestured to the sweeping spindle staircase. "This home has five bedrooms, five baths, and five fireplaces. It's the opposite of a perfect flip house."

"Nevertheless, lead the way. There're two more floors to check out."

After he'd inspected the upstairs bathrooms and admired the worn brass hardware on the master suite's mahogany double doors, they made their way downstairs.

When they reached the foyer, he glanced up from his cell phone and said, "I want to make an offer."

She shuffled back two steps. "You're joking ... right?" Her gaze shifted to the entrance. She'd made a serious mistake in mentioning this house to him.

"I never joke about real estate."

"This home"—she swept out her hands—"is a money pit."

"Which is why Rob and I will buy the property for the land."

Candee's heart stopped beating.

"We'll demolish the house," he added.

Her house, she wanted to shout. *Her* land for disadvantaged children. She'd envisioned beagle puppies cavorting across the lawn, perhaps an acre set aside for a working farm. Children needed to connect with nature. It was time to get them away from technology and back to values that really mattered.

And music. The music room off the kitchen would reverberate with glorious sounds again.

Teddy faced her. "Anything the matter?"

There was kindness in his gaze, interest on his handsome features. Should she share her ideas with a man she'd known for less than two hours—a man who was bent on destroying those very same ideas? A man who'd held her hand in his strong grip and gazed at the Victorian with the same wonder and appreciation as she had?

Struggling to hold onto her composure, she reminded herself she was a professional. Besides, this house was nothing like what he was looking for.

She lifted her chin. "Not a thing."

Lightly, he touched her cheek, his gesture completely unexpected. "I understand how you feel about a house like this. It's very beautiful, but beyond repair."

Turning away, she quickly dabbed at her eyes. She settled into the tune she'd known the past two years: no matter how sincere, how charming, men couldn't be trusted. Better to hold him at a polite distance and keep her plans to herself. He'd soon be gone back to Miami.

"Are you sure you're okay?" he asked.

She feigned her brightest smile. "Of course."

He waited a beat, then silently followed her, standing on the porch while she locked the front door.

"Any idea what the current bid is? You mentioned under fifty thousand."

Candee rubbed her temples. A quick search on the Internet would spew all the information he'd need to place a bid.

"Twenty thousand dollars," she finally said. "And bidding ends in three weeks."

So many mistakes today, beginning by answering the phone. 1-800-CUPID. Hah!

"Then I'll offer thirty thousand dollars," he said.

An uneasy quiet descended. A cold breeze brushed across her cheeks.

"The auction accepts bids in twenty-thousand dollar-increments," she said.

"Then I'll bid forty thousand, which is still under my fifty-thousand-dollar budget."

"The bank may not accept a lowball offer." Her remark was nonsensical, since she was hoping the bank would accept her offer, because twenty thousand dollars was all she had. She glanced at Teddy's determined stance. Surely there was a way to convince him not to bid. However, thirty years of proper Southern behavior stopped her from saying more.

"I can offer all cash," he said. "Plus, my partner and I can close immediately. On a foreclosure, the bank will take every-thing into consideration."

"Don't you want to walk the property? If you're interested in the land, there are building requirements and permits—"

He reached into his pocket and handed her a business card. "I do this for a living, Candee. I know all about due dili-gence." He gave a lazy grin. "And there's another clause, which can either make or break the deal."

She fisted one hand on her hip. "The bank should just hand over the house to you?"

"A definite bonus." He laughed, rich and full. "I'm hoping my lovely realtor will grant me the pleasure of her company at dinner."

"I can't." Her refusal was quick, a knee-jerk reaction. She hadn't dated in two years and wouldn't start now, especially with a tycoon investor who assumed that by flaunting the cash in his pocket, he could take her castle in the air away from her.

"Not even for a slice of pizza? I don't know my way around Roses yet."

She retreated a step. "Tony's Pizza on Main Street is always open. You can spot the red and green awning a mile away."

"Are you saying no, Candee?"

"Is my refusal a deal breaker, Teddy?"

"Not if I can get this property for under fifty thousand dollars."

"If you decide to bid, you'll have to wait three weeks to find out if you've won."

His gaze lingered on her face. "Some things are worth waiting for."

CHAPTER FOUR

*T*eddy's cell phone buzzed on the nightstand in his hotel room. Awake anyway, he answered it and heard a recognizable woman's voice.

"Teddy?"

"Yvonne?" He peered at the clock on the nightstand. "You realize it's three a.m.?"

"Are you awake?"

He pushed a hand through his hair. "Should I be?"

"It's nine in the morning here in Madrid."

"I'm not in Spain," he countered.

"Such a shame you aren't with me." A long feminine sigh. "I'll never get used to the time difference. Look, my network in the States wants me in Madrid another few weeks to cover the recent drought. Water levels in the reservoirs are abnormally low, and they're aiming for a human-interest story to boost ratings and land a prime-time slot."

Teddy had met Yvonne—an attractive woman with honeyed skin, her thinly arched black brows offset by a pixie cut of platinum-blonde hair—when he'd been offered a weekly television segment featuring tidbits on flipping homes. His fifteen minutes of fame had lasted, well, fifteen minutes. His relationship with Yvonne was going on five months, although he hardly ever saw her. Her job involved a great deal of travel, and he wasn't diligent about keeping in touch with her. He wasn't adaptable to the ever-changing elasticity of dating a woman he saw only twice a month.

He extended the expected congratulatory remarks. Compliments were a prerequisite when dating Yvonne Evette. She was a career woman bent on reaching the top, although what 'the top' was had yet to be determined. Currently, it meant an anchor position on a major American network.

After good-byes, he clicked off his phone and shifted restlessly on his narrow bed. The previous morning when he'd arrived at the Roses Hotel and realized the four-star rating wasn't accurate, he'd debated about sitting on the bed, much less lying on it. Still, he'd pulled back the bedspread, flopped down, and peered at a stain on the ceiling, trying not to ponder how it got there, for it certainly wasn't a water stain.

Now, in the darkened room, he punched a pillow and rolled onto his side.

Night after night since his brother's death, sleep had been elusive.

That's what happened when two brothers grew up together facing the shared futility of scarcity and endless beatings from their drug-addled father. Nothing was left of the Winchester heritage except the old Florida farm, the rundown homestead sitting on two acres of land at the end of a county road. And no matter how wealthy Teddy became, his roots were fixed in poverty.

Fortunately, his brother Christian had held onto the farm after Christian's wife died a year earlier, refurbishing the place and attempting to grow citrus fruit. The crops hadn't produced one grapefruit, as far as Teddy knew. Neither he nor

Christian had the knack for farming, and Christian had always struggled when it came to financial success.

Lately, Teddy found himself talking to his late brother: *Christian, should I do this, should I do that? I'm a bachelor. Am I the best choice as Joseph's legal guardian?*

Christian had been an exemplary father. How was Teddy expected to fill those impressive shoes? Perhaps he should marry, he pondered, providing a stable home for Joseph as his brother had done.

Turning onto his back and linking his hands behind his head he thought about Yvonne—her suggestive words, her open invitations, her sultry voice. However, he didn't want Yvonne. His mind traveled instead to *Miss* Candee Contando, the beautiful realtor with the creamy complexion, a mass of red hair framing her face and long legs that went on forever.

Her realty skills were non-existent. When he'd pressed her for details about any property under fifty thousand, she'd hesitated for a lengthy spell before answering. When they'd stood together and stared at the Victorian, he'd had to fight down the impulse to kiss her while holding her hand. She was gorgeous and witty, with a cool no-nonsense façade. And somehow, he knew she'd require a sizable amount of convincing to date him.

He didn't know the reason for his next decision. He only knew he wanted to see her again.

He'd visit her office first thing Monday morning with some excuse, and then invite her to lunch. Perhaps he'd bid on the property with her assistance.

Envisioning Candee's beautiful face, he drifted off to sleep.

"*P*izza?" Desiree repeated. "The guy's taking you out for pizza?"

Candee smoothed the collar of her royal-blue silk blouse. She wore an outfit appropriate for dinner at the fancy country club her sister belonged to—the silk blouse and a black pencil skirt, and black stilettos.

"If you recall," she said, "I'm not going."

"Was he bald?"

Candee sipped her water. "No. His hair is dark and wavy."

"Short?"

"Wrong again. He's at least six feet tall. If anything, he's exceptionally handsome." Her heart gave a peculiar little pitch as she remembered his outrageous smile when he'd asked if she wanted to join him in the basement.

"Married?"

"No, although he talked about his nephew."

Desiree reached for her crystal wineglass filled with a local red wine. "Rich?"

"I checked his business listing on the Internet. R and T Realty in Miami is legit."

A teasing smile tilted Desiree's lips. "Then why would you refuse his offer to go out for pizza?"

Because all her energies were focused on the Victorian house, Candee wanted to say. Because she wasn't ready for a relationship.

"Because he's placing a bid on the Langrone mansion so he can tear it down," she responded aloud.

Desiree beckoned to a waiter who immediately splashed more water into the women's glasses. "Has he lost his mind like you have?"

Candee assessed her perfectly coiffed sister. Desiree was her usual stunning self, her blonde hair caught at the crown of her head with a glittering rhinestone fastener.

Forking a piece of lettuce, she replied, "Perhaps that's how these high-roller investor types go about flips."

"Once the house is torn down, what's he going to do with a vacant five-acre lot?"

"He didn't explain." Candee pushed her half-eaten meal of salad, grilled salmon and roasted red potatoes aside. "Who spends thousands of dollars to tear down a beautiful piece of property which should be preserved, not destroyed?"

Desiree finished her wine and set her glass to the side. "His reasons might be good ones."

"Well, he won't have the opportunity to tell me. I won't be seeing him again."

"Give him a chance. He sounds utterly gorgeous. Call him."

Candee leaned back and crossed her arms. "I've never called a guy in my life."

"Your life, your decision." Desiree's gaze traveled through the expansive dining room. "Did I mention the club is having a Valentine's Day silent auction and dinner dance? I remember how beautifully you helped me decorate the dining room two years ago. We filled champagne glasses with candy hearts—and the chocolate fondue was fabulous!"

Candee faked a glibness she didn't feel. "You're referring to the night my ex walked out on me for another woman."

"You'll be happier if you don't dwell on the past," Desiree said. "Besides, you'd discussed ending your relationship with George two months before the actual breakup. Focus on what's ahead and let the past stay where it belongs."

Before Candee could answer, Desiree trilled a giggle and waved. "Scott's here, the man who took me out last night."

Candee peered over her shoulder. "The guy with the blond crewcut sitting alone at a table near the bar?"

"Yes. I mentioned we were eating here tonight, and he said he might join us for dessert, and then we discussed he might bring a friend ... umm ... for you. The friend's name is Allen Allen."

"You planned to set me up on a blind date?" Candee half-stood. "Thanks, but no thanks."

"What's wrong with meeting a man for coffee and dessert? Maybe we can double date for the Valentine dance."

"The dance I'm not attending," Candee reminded.

Desiree peered in Scott's direction. "I don't see anyone with him." She frowned, then pulled her vibrating cell phone from her handbag. She flashed Scott a smile and read his text aloud. "Allen heard the weather might take a turn for the worse, so he decided not to come."

"The guy's name really is Allen Allen?"

"He practices law in a neighboring town. He and Scott went to school together."

Candee was no longer listening. She was peering out the nearest window, assessing the weather. The earlier light drizzle was turning to sleet, and she thought it prudent to leave sooner rather than later. Within a few minutes she was pulling on her jacket, a faux fur capelet, and Desiree was sharing Scott's table with him.

As Candee prepared to exit, she walked straight into a tall attractive man wearing navy pants, a striped polo shirt, and a gray sport coat.

"Candee? What are you doing here?" Teddy's gaze slid slowly up her, from her stilettos and slim-fitting skirt to her silk blouse, finally stopping at her face.

She fingered her gold cross earrings. "May I ask you the same question?"

"My partner has a reciprocal agreement with private clubs around the country. Since you refused my pizza offer last night ..." He gave an appreciative male smile. "You know, you're a knockout when you're all dressed up."

Heat flushed her cheeks. "Thanks for the ... compliment?"

"I mean, you're a beautiful woman whether you're wearing jeans or—"

Now the flush warmed her ears. "Well, thanks again. I was just leaving."

"Me too. I ordered takeout food and forgot forks." He flourished a bag with the country club's logo as proof, then glanced out the window by the front door. "Roses certainly has unpredictable weather."

"It's not usually like this." She attempted to brush past him. "Whereas Florida's weather is predictably hot and sunny."

"Especially Miami." He grinned. "Where are you parked?"

"I came with my sister, Desiree, who's ditched me. She prefers to drink coffee with her latest conquest, a new lawyer at her firm." Candee glanced over her shoulder at the bar area. Desiree was watching her, and she grinned and offered a thumbs-up.

Candee didn't respond, turning back to Teddy. "She and her newest conquest had planned a blind date for me, although Allen Allen, another lawyer, decided I wasn't worth the effort of driving in bad weather."

Teddy's dark eyebrows quirked. "This guy's first and last name are the same?"

"Yes." She surprised herself by adding, "It would have been my first date in two years, although I would've refused."

"His loss is my gain. I'll take you home."

Absolutely not.

"No, no." Candee shook her head while securing her capelet. "I planned to call a taxi."

Teddy gestured toward his pickup truck. "I'm parked at the curb. And your vocabulary might improve if you substituted yes for no once in a while."

"I can't. Really—"

"Say yes."

No use in arguing with him. His references had checked out and he wasn't a total stranger. She smiled. "All right. I don't live far from here."

"Much better."

With his hand on her elbow, he guided her outside to his truck, opening the passenger door and helping her up and in. Her tight skirt didn't allow for much climbing, and she shifted into the seat, hoping her skirt wouldn't ride up her thighs.

It did, and judging from his appreciative smile, he noticed.

"My address is 121 Juniper Street," she said, after she'd adjusted her skirt to a more proper length.

"I'll plug it into my cell phone."

She glanced at his profile as he slid into the driver's seat. Way too attractive, she thought, in a roguish way.

"What about your silverware for the takeout?" she asked.

He flashed a boyish grin, displaying even white teeth. "The club's signature hamburger can be eaten with human fingers, and there's a supply of paper napkins in my truck's glove compartment."

"You're well-equipped."

For a fleeting second, his gaze turned somber. "I try, although sometimes life throws some unexpected curves."

At close range, she noted a scar below his right eye. It certainly didn't affect his good looks, but she wondered if it indicated some of those unexpected curves life had thrown at him.

CHAPTER FIVE

*T*he sleet came faster, making visibility difficult. Still, Teddy seemed to recognize where they were as they neared the turn-off for Thompson Lane.

"You know the code for the lockbox, right?" Teddy asked.

"Yes, I have it memorized," she said.

"Mind if we stop there first? I'd meant to check the water heater yesterday. In the excitement of falling through the floor, I forgot."

She caught her lower lip with her teeth to stop from blurting out. He wanted to see *her* Victorian again?

"The weather—" She gestured theatrically to the icy roads.

"I have 4-wheel drive."

"Did you offer me a ride tonight in order to get into the house again?"

He slowed the truck, studying her for a couple heartbeats, and she attributed his silence to his interest in the Victorian. "I had no idea you were dining at the country club this evening," he said.

There was enough truth in his statement to make her

cheeks burn. Still, she persisted. "But when you did, you seized the opportunity."

He offered a disarming chuckle. "Perhaps that was my second thought."

She couldn't help a reciprocal grin. Truly, the guy was impossible. "And what was your first thought?"

He glanced at her, and for a moment, she was caught in the spell of his irresistible dark eyes. "How lucky I was to see you twice in two days," he said softly.

A faint smile touched her mouth. She stared out the windshield at the falling sleet, trying to decide if he was harmlessly flirting with her or telling the truth.

"There's no electricity at the house, Teddy. It will be freezing and dark."

"There's a gas fireplace in the living room. I called the gas company this morning. The meter is running as the gas was never switched off." The truck slid on the slick road. He reduced his speed again, gripping the steering wheel and focusing on the taillights ahead of them. "And I keep extra flashlights and candles in my truck."

"Are you always prepared, regardless of the circumstances?"

His lips twitched. "I try to think of everything."

When they reached the circular driveway, he inched his truck along it and slid to a stop. At night, the Victorian loomed majestic and mammoth, set against the stormy winter sky. She imagined smoke curling from all five chimneys, the welcoming fireplaces blazing in the enormous hearths.

"This house is a proverbial jewel in the rough," she murmured.

"Yes, it is." Teddy's expression softened. He got out of the truck, hoisted a knapsack over his shoulders, and then opened the passenger door for her.

"I could get used to this," she said.

He assisted her out of the truck and took her hand. "Used to what?"

"Being treated like a lady."

He blinked. "Is there any other way to treat a woman?"

Unfortunately, yes, there were plenty of other ways.

She drew in a sharp breath, remembering the verbal abuse she'd suffered with George. How he'd yell to silence her when she didn't agree with him; his chiding, "Come on, can't you take a joke, Candee?" after he'd made fun of her cooking, or her clothes, or her mannerisms. Their relationship had sent her into a tailspin of self-doubt and self-preservation.

Teddy interrupted her musings. "Shall I carry you up the stairs and over the threshold?"

"I can walk perfectly fine on my own."

She took one step and skated forward.

He slipped an arm around her shoulders. "Just in case, I'll keep you steady."

"Stilettos weren't made for walking," she joked, accepting his embrace and leaning into his solid chest as her heels crunched along the crusty ice.

He chuckled. "I'm not complaining."

They walked to the house under an onslaught of bone-chilling, wind-blown sleet.

Teddy was proving to be a gentleman, she mused, holding her securely and concerned about her welfare, in a fast-paced era where common courtesies were oftentimes forgotten. Gratefully, she smiled up at him.

When they reached the porch, she punched the code into the lockbox, extracted the key and unlocked the door.

He flicked on his phone flashlight and steered them to the living room. "I'll get the gas fireplace running and then we'll have dinner." He pulled a blanket from his knapsack and set it on the floor, gesturing her to sit. Then he placed his gray sport coat beside her.

"You can't light the fireplace and you shouldn't eat in here. The bank owns the house—we don't." She removed her capelet and installed herself on the blanket with her legs straight out, her tight black skirt tucked securely around them. "There are laws, Teddy ..."

"If anyone asks, you're my realtor and I'm the man buying the house."

"And as your realtor, may I remind you that you're making a mistake by even thinking about purchasing a home in such poor shape? This isn't a wise investment for a house-flipper."

"I'm tearing it down, remember?" He walked to the fireplace and held the pilot button down for a couple minutes. A flame flickered, and the fire soon glowed, warming the room.

She sighed. "What else is in your knapsack?"

"Soy candles." He brought out a tidy boxed candle set along with a book of matches. He lit the candles and placed them on the fireplace mantel. "The box described these candles as part of the 'jasmine and cedar wood atmosphere collection.'"

"Well then, they're perfect," she said, amused.

He sat beside her, opened his takeout box and held up a massive hamburger. "Ah, dinner by candlelight."

"No dessert? I love caramels coated in chocolate."

"I'll bring caramels next time. Dark or milk chocolate?"

"Dark." She chortled. "Bring those, and how could I refuse?"

"Hopefully, you can't refuse anything I offer." His teasing laugh was potent, and his affectionate appraisal made her heart rate rise. Along with the aroma of the cedar candles, she inhaled Teddy's clean scent, all male, and the air around them heated.

They fell into companionable silence, as he shared his crispy fries and had a bite of his hamburger. On top of the dinner she'd already eaten, she was consuming more calories than she normally ate in two days.

When they were finished, Teddy picked up the napkins strewn beside them. "What do you do when you're not selling real estate?" he asked.

"I volunteer at the Roses no-kill animal shelter every Sunday." She wiped her fingers on a napkin. "And I work part-time at the hardware store in town, since I like making things out of wood. My foster family's business was working with wood."

His hands stilled. "Your foster family?"

"When we were teenagers, my sister and I were removed from our home and placed into the state welfare system as foster children."

Once she blurted out the words, Candee chided herself. What had compelled her to divulge so much information? If she'd blinked, she would have missed the kind interest clouding Teddy's face before he replaced his expression with a teasing grin.

"And what do you make out of wood? Should I book you a spot on the home improvement channel?" he asked.

"I'd wait about fifty years if I were you. I'm not ready for my own television show." She fixed her stare on the burning gas logs in the fireplace. "I made a detailed dollhouse once with my foster father, complete with a rocking chair measuring three inches." She paused as tears threatened. "I still have that chair."

He kept his gaze on her face. "Care to tell me about your foster family?"

"Which one?"

"There was more than one?"

"We were shuffled to five different families." Her throat tightened as the memories washed over her. "The agency urged each foster family to keep us, and then the family would decide not to adopt."

Two teenage girls with no parents hadn't been worthy of love or a stable home.

Teddy was watching her closely. "Go on," he said quietly.

She swallowed. "The last family Desiree and I were placed with ended up being our 'forever' family." Candee commended herself on her steady tone. "We attended church together, and in the evening we often sang hymns around their old upright piano while I attempted to plunk out the tunes."

"I'm impressed." He considered her with open admiration. "You make dollhouses and play the piano and volunteer at a no-kill animal shelter. That is, when you're not selling real estate."

He'd turned the conversation away from her past, and she was appreciative. Most days, she secured her childhood memories in a protected compartment in her mind. Sitting with Teddy, who seemed so attuned to her, she felt comfortable and safe.

She half smiled. "I don't do any of those things remarkably well, except volunteering at the animal shelter. Animals love you no matter who you are or your background."

He shook his head. "I've never had time for animals."

"Doesn't your four-year-old nephew live with you?"

"Yes, although it's only been for the past few months, and we're still getting used to each other. Rob's watching him now while I'm away. Joseph rides horses on weekends at an equestrian center near Miami, and now he wants a horse."

"He'll probably beg for a dog at some point, too."

Teddy chuckled. "He already has asked."

Get him a rescue dog, preferably a beagle, she wanted to encourage. Although, seeing the closed expression on Teddy's face, she didn't pursue the subject.

"Do you read music?" she asked.

"I'm no Beethoven, although I can keep a steady beat on a timpani drum." He stood and gathered their trash in the carryout bag. "I'd like to go with you to the animal shelter—if I'm properly invited. You volunteer every Sunday?"

"Immediately after church."

He paused, then winked. "I'm waiting for an invite."

She couldn't help laughing. "The shelter needs all the help it can get, although volunteers must first attend an orientation, give references and then commit to a certain length of time."

"Can you vouch for me? I'll be living in Roses for the next few weeks."

"All right."

"Flexible hours?" he asked with amusement.

She grinned. "Absolutely."

"Then I'll assist in any way I can." He pulled a battery-operated transistor radio out of his knapsack. Turning it on, he fiddled with the dial until he found a crackly station playing 80's music. "Would you like to dance, Candee?"

"You want to dance—now?"

"You're still shivering a little." He offered a playful smile. "It's better to move around when you're cold."

"I'm not shivering," she informed him. "And I haven't danced with a man in forever."

Any further protest died on her lips as he pulled her to her feet.

"I can't remember the last time I danced with a woman, either." He placed his arm around her back. "Although I remember I liked it."

Candee silenced another protest. *Why not dance? The entire evening had a one-of-a-kind, storybook quality to it.*

"Unchained Melody" came on.

"I love the Righteous Brothers," she announced.

Teddy smoothed his fingers across her shoulders and pulled her closer. "I noticed when we were riding in your car yesterday."

They swayed in step to the enchanting words of the ballad about lonely rivers flowing and sighing.

The glow of the fireplace, dancing slowly with this strikingly handsome man, made her forget the previous two years of heartache and aloneness and dateless evenings.

"This music is in twelve eight time," she said.

He kept his fingers joined with hers. "It's beautiful."

With a quiet sigh, she submerged herself in the melody of the timeless song. The minutes passed and she lost track of the following medley of classic songs. She simply relaxed against Teddy's chest and allowed herself to experience the reassuring presence of his solid body against hers. His heart thudded in a steady meter and her own heart felt strange, beating oh-so-fast.

"Candee?" He lifted her chin. "If I was that guy with the same first and last names, I'd have rented a snowplow to meet you at the country club tonight."

His deep brown eyes darkened. Her body warmed with anticipation as his hands drifted down her shoulders, pressing her nearer.

It was there, an invisible thread drawing them together.

Her mind warned: It couldn't be, not after knowing him for a day.

But it was.

She knew he was going to kiss her, and she met his insistent lips with an eagerness she'd never known. He kissed her slowly, thoroughly. The strength of his powerful body molded intimately to hers, bringing her to life. The longer the kiss went on, the more she responded, straining to be nearer him.

The doorbell rang.

Teddy broke the kiss. "Are you expecting dinner guests?"

He tipped up her chin. Affection and desire smoldered in his gaze as his thumbs stroked her heated cheeks.

Her hands flattened against his polo shirt and she rested her head on his chest. "Not unless they brought chocolate."

He laughed. "It must be the wind."

The odd chime of the doorbell ringing a second time prompted her to pull from his arms.

A moment afterward, the front door opened sending a blast of cold air into the living room.

"Anyone home?" a gruff voice called out.

A pair of heavy footsteps tromped down the hallway, and an elderly man with gray hair appeared in the living room doorway. With one hand, he pushed up a pair of thick glasses. With the other, he raised a sizable wooden baseball bat.

"Who are you two?" he demanded.

Candee retreated a step. "Mr. Dunworthy?"

"Candee Contando? What are you doing here?" The aging man hobbled into the room, using the baseball bat as a cane. "I saw candles flickering. I figured it was teenagers up to mischief and decided to walk down here to see for myself."

"Mr. Dunworthy." Teddy came forward. "Candee was showing me the house."

"At this hour?" Up close, the dark age spots on the man's face showed prominently. He squinted and stared at Teddy. "You live around here?"

"No. I'm from Florida, actually. My name is Teddy Winchester. I live in Miami and I'm an investor." Teddy extended his hand.

Mr. Dunworthy placed the baseball bat on the floor and the men shook hands. "I'm Charles Dunworthy. I live two doors down and I'm your basic nosy neighbor.

CHAPTER SIX

*T*he following day, Candee attended church services. Upon returning to her apartment for a quick lunch, she checked her cell phone. Teddy had texted her.

Happy Sunday, his text read. *Planning to volunteer at the animal shelter this afternoon?*

She glanced at her watch—half past noon. *Yes*, she texted back. *On my way now.*

Can I join u?

Teddy was persistent and apparently interested in her. He was so good-looking and not at all arrogant. His manner was compelling, gentle, yet with an aura of control. She so regretted that Mr. Dunworthy had interrupted their one kiss.

She suppressed a grin and texted back. *All hands are welcome.*

She sent him the address and then changed into a plaid flannel shirt, old faded jeans, black leather boots, and a light navy jacket. After pulling her hair into a casual pony tail, she tied the green paisley scarf around her neck. Despite the freezing weather the previous evening, the sky was a brilliant

Carolina blue, the sun efficiently melting any sleet left on the ground.

Candee recognized Teddy's pickup as soon as she drove into the shelter's parking lot. Lounging against his truck, he displayed an easy charm, looking exceedingly handsome wearing dark jeans, his olive-green vest zipped over a black T-shirt. He was ruggedly fit, his arm muscles taut and hard.

He strode to her car, his boots crunching on the graveled parking lot, and had her door open before she'd taken her key out of the ignition.

"Did you attend services this morning?" His slow, lazy smile made her shamelessly wonder how it would feel to kiss him again.

As she got out of the car, she drew a long breath to steady her fluttering pulse and focused on the simple wood-sided entrance door. "Yes, and the sermon was amazing. The pastor spoke about how grace is the way to heaven and faith is the route we choose to take. Do you attend a church?"

His nodded. "A contemporary church in Florida. They stream their services online and I watched on my computer early this morning before I called my nephew."

"How is he?"

"He sounded happy. I'll fly to Miami next weekend to see him. He's having a good time with Rob." He peered past her at the modern concrete and brick building. "How long is our shift?"

"Four hours. And an application is required."

"Done," he said. "I attended the orientation already and used your name as a reference. Was that okay?"

"Of course." She paused. "When you texted me, were you already at the shelter?"

He shifted. "I guess I was."

"You guess? You blithely did nothing while I texted directions?"

He raised a hand. "Guilty as charged. Last night you invited me to join you, remember?" Grinning, he took her hand. "Shall we go inside?"

She liked his easy-going sense of humor. In the spirt of friendly bantering, she teased, "Do you want to clean the crates, walk the dogs or stuff envelopes?"

"I have a choice?"

She chuckled. "It depends on whether you want to sit or stand. I prefer walking the dogs and love being outside."

He gazed down at her and squeezed her hand. "I'll go wherever you go." His words hung significantly in the crisp January breeze.

The next four hours passed amidst amiable sparring and chatter, with Candee teasing Teddy that he was supposed to be walking the dogs—the dogs weren't supposed to be walking him.

Dusk had fallen by the time Teddy was placing the last dog back in its enclosure as Candee explained the shelter's protocol and safety procedures to help limit the transfer of disease. For the next fifteen minutes, they assisted last-minute customers with animal visitations.

As they got ready to leave, Candee called out a jovial good-bye to Agnes, another volunteer.

"Will you and your boyfriend be back here next week?" Agnes asked.

Candee blinked.

She was coming to value Teddy's friendship ... but *boyfriend?* No, no, no. She wasn't ready to open her heart to another relationship—because Teddy would leave, like her parents, like the foster families, like George. Absolutely, she wanted to build a social life for herself again, but not at the expense of another heartbreak.

She took a steadying breath, resolve firmly in control. "Teddy and I met three days ago, Agnes. I'm his ... realtor."

"Oh." The woman studied them. "You two just look like you're together. I assumed you were a couple."

From the corner of her eye, Candee noted Teddy's quirked eyebrow, although he said nothing. She glanced at her hand in the crook of his arm. It felt natural, although she didn't remember placing her hand there.

As they walked away, Teddy whispered in her ear. "Well, that opens up a landslide of potential for us, doesn't it? Now will you join me for dinner?" Leaning over, he opened her car door.

"I'm at my realty office by eight o' clock on Monday morning." She bit her lip, debating his invitation. "In the afternoon, I work at the hardware store."

"I promise to get you home early." His grin was wide, his gaze glinted with merriment. "Say yes, because we're a couple now. Just ask Agnes."

"I never said—"

Lightly, he kissed her forehead. "We've been on our feet for hours. Don't you need nourishment? Eating a few slices of pizza won't take long."

Her hand hovered uncertainly above her car keys before she agreed. "I'm starved, actually."

The sun was descending as they arrived at Tony's pizzeria on Main Street. They parked their cars near the entrance, and Teddy came around to open her car door.

She smiled as he complimented her, citing how magnificent she was with animals and how much he prized her nurturing manner.

He gestured to the entrance of the pizzeria. "I made reservations. I didn't want us to sit around waiting for a pager to go off. Especially since you go to work early in the morning."

The soft tenderness in his deep voice took her breath away.

Was it wrong for her to enjoy being well-treated? she questioned herself. Teddy made her feel special—listening attentively while she spoke, sensitive to her moods and attuned to her emotions. He obviously cared, showing initiative and planning ahead so she'd have a decent night's rest.

He took her hand as they walked into the pizzeria.

Mouth-watering scents of freshly cooked pasta, pizza, garlic, and oregano drifted through the darkly-lit restaurant. A portly woman, looking just like an Italian grandmother, escorted them to a table near a cheery fireplace. The woman was dressed in pressed black slacks and a turtleneck sweater, with "Tony's" stitched in red on the collar. A spiked-haired pizza maker stood in front of an open brick oven tossing pizza dough in the air and then covering the circle of dough with tomato sauce, pepperoni, and cheese.

Candee took in a deep breath. "Italian is my favorite food in all the world."

"*M*ine, too," Teddy agreed. As he pulled out a chair for Candee, he took in Tony's traditional decor—red and white checkered tablecloths, Italian statues and grapevines, the muted atmospheric lighting enhanced by votive candles at each table.

He took a seat, and they accepted menus from the waitress, a sandy-haired teen who seemed far more interested in the pizza tosser than in her customers.

Teddy perused the menu. "I love anything with the word pizza."

"Tossed salad is a nutritious alternative," she said.

After they were both served, Candee tucked into her salad while Teddy loaded up his plate with three slices of Margherita pizza.

"Do you have a favorite dog?"

He stopped in midchew to consider her unexpected question. "I came across many breeds today and it's hard to say. You?"

She smiled, but there was a hint of sadness to it. "I love beagles."

He was about to ask why when the waitress appeared. "More water? Coffee?"

"Black coffee for me," Candee said.

"Two cups, please," Teddy said.

A few minutes later the waitress set steaming cups of coffee on the table, cleared their empty plates, and encouraged them to order dessert.

"You haven't eaten any pizza yet," Teddy said. "There are two slices left."

"Box up what's left," Candee said to the waitress. "Teddy, you can have the leftovers for a midnight snack."

He laughed. "Since I professed my love for pizza earlier, I therefore have a good excuse for eating most of it." He gazed at Candee, who was twirling the ends of her thick red hair. He knew he was monopolizing her weekend, but she had been utterly enchanting while she'd handled the animals, treating every dog with respect and compassion, sensitive to the different breeds. She'd walked the dogs alongside him, hips swaying, her tall willowy figure provocative, laughing out loud at his knock-knock jokes.

Finally, he'd met someone who appreciated his sense of humor.

He loathed giving her up quite yet, and he planned to ask for a coffee refill when the waitress came back.

As the waitress went around the corner to box up the pizza and flirt with the pizza tosser, Teddy leaned forward. "Why do you love beagles, Candee?"

She broke eye contact and shrugged. "Long story."

"I'm a good listener." He scuffed his chair closer to the

table. "Last night you mentioned your 'forever' family. I'm assuming the two stories go together. Care to elaborate?"

She cupped her hands around her coffee cup as the waitress set the boxed pizza by Teddy. He waited while Candee sipped coffee and fixed her gaze on the crackling fire in the fireplace. Setting the cup down, she said, "The Johnsons encouraged Desiree and me to attend college."

"They sound like good people. Are you still in touch with them?"

"Six years ago, they moved to Chicago. I haven't seen them since I graduated from college. We still email, and I hope to visit them someday."

"What about your other foster families?" he asked gently. "You mentioned there were five families altogether."

She waved a hand dismissively. "Why would you be interested in hearing the sad story of my childhood?"

"Because I'm interested in you and everything about you."

She blushed and slowly exhaled. "Desiree and I encouraged each other every time we moved, assuring each other everything was fine, but it wasn't, you know? Between the ages of twelve and seventeen, we'd lived in four foster homes. New parents were complete strangers to us, and every house had its own set of rules—where to sleep, how to dress, what to eat, chores that had to be done."

Reaching out, he traced his finger along the curve of her cheek. "Those must have been very hard and scary years for two teenage girls."

The smile she offered quickly faded. "I always felt like a misfit. We didn't do anything normal teenagers did. No sleepovers, no driver's licenses—only a continuous series of knowing we were outsiders wherever we went."

She paused and stared down at her coffee. She'd hardly drunk any.

He took her silence as consent that she'd continue, and waited.

She gazed out the window at a cluster of clouds sitting low in the sky, then shifted her gaze to his. "Looking back, the hardest part was the beginning. I can still visualize my sister and me packing all our belongings into green trash bags the day we were taken from our home. I was twelve at the time. Desiree was fourteen."

"May I ask why you were put in foster care?"

She stared past him. "Our parents were declared unfit, and the state deemed it necessary for my sister and me to live in a safer place." She fidgeted with her gold earrings. "Although I didn't understand at the time, in hindsight I see there was no other choice. Our parents died soon after we were removed, and the doctors blamed their deaths on substance abuse."

"I'm sorry." He took her cold, fidgeting hands in his. "And now you've grown into a beautiful young woman. From my brief glimpse of your sister, she seems to be doing well. She's a lawyer?"

"And a good one, advocating for children's rights," Candee responded brightly. "I'm committed to making a difference in children's lives too. I have a plan that includes a rambling property with five acres, where children can safely go after school and learn music and play with dogs and finish their homework and eat healthy snacks ..." Her voice trailed off.

"I applaud you." He grinned approvingly and glided his thumbs over her hands. "What's your plan?"

It was just like her to want to help others, he thought. He imagined her as a kind and caring mother—a perfect mother for Joseph.

Perfect for Joseph and perfect for him. He scowled at himself, surprised the idea had drifted into his mind of its own accord. With a long sigh, he acknowledged the truth.

Candee was an extraordinary woman, compassionate and warm-hearted. At thirty-two years old, he'd never felt such an instant attraction to a woman. After knowing her for only a few days, he was already half in love with her.

Perhaps fate had brought them together.

"You might as well know all the facts, Teddy," she was saying.

His thumbs froze on her hands in midstroke. He made himself resume, collecting his thoughts before asking, "What facts?"

She pulled her hands from his. "I should have addressed the situation and told you everything on Friday." Her voice was so low, he strained to hear her.

"Tell me what?" He leaned in closer, promising himself that whatever these facts were, it didn't matter.

For a fleeting moment, she closed her eyes, but then she pushed her shoulders back and squarely met his gaze. "The twenty-thousand dollar bid on the Victorian? It's my bid. I'm planning to live there and renovate the downstairs space, making it an after-school day care for disadvantaged children." Her voice caught. She paused before her words rushed out. "Therefore, I'd appreciate if you took your money elsewhere, preferably Miami, because the Victorian is taken."

CHAPTER SEVEN

*T*aken? The Victorian was taken?

Teddy jerked off his vest and threw it on the worn oak chair in his hotel room. He approached the window and gazed out at a thick black sky. In the distance, the twinkling lights of shops in the town square beckoned. Somewhere near, a church bell tolled the hour.

He tapped his hands together and spoke softly to his brother. "Really, Christian? Candee bid on the irreparable property in Roses that I'm interested in?"

With a heavy sigh, Teddy shoved his hands into his jean pockets. There were few moments in his life when he recalled being at a loss for words, but he definitely hadn't known what to say when Candee announced her plans. He'd mumbled something about having no idea she'd wanted the property, paid the restaurant bill while acknowledging her 'thank you,' then matched her swift steps as he walked her to her car.

At first, he'd been angry. Why hadn't she simply told him? True, he'd been insistent about seeing the property. However, if the Victorian meant that much to her—which it apparently did—she should have never taken him to see it.

His anger had evaporated on his drive back to the hotel. In retrospect, her intentions explained her hesitancy, her efforts to talk him out of buying it himself. And if he hadn't been so intent on purchasing a bargain, he would have spotted what was clear in hindsight—she loved the house. He'd clearly seen her wistful gaze when she'd held his hand and stared at the property with him.

He shook his head, berating himself. Here he thought she was the world's worst realtor. Instead, she was trying to protect her investment, and perhaps her heart. Her life had been filled with trauma and transience, yet in what he recognized already as true Candee style, her aspiration was to transform the house into a safe environment for disadvantaged children.

His head-strong, courageous Candee.

He recalled the night before, the candlelight living room and her amused, "You want to dance—now?" After the music started, she'd snuggled close, her soft curves pressed against him. She'd felt warm and responsive, and the mere touch of her hands on his shoulders had heated his pulse. Just thinking about the tumultuous highs of the past three days made the short time they'd spent together all the more significant.

He sensed she was beginning to care for him too. Nonetheless, common sense warned that love had no place in his life. He owned a thriving real estate business in Florida and had a nephew who needed him there.

There was no reason he couldn't continue seeing her, though, his heart encouraged. All that stood between them was the house and a distance of over seven hundred miles. Both easily remedied, he assured himself, between phone calls and Skype, although his conscience nagged about how he didn't do well in long-distance relationships.

With a low exhale, he turned away from the window.

Before they'd departed, he'd pressed a kiss to her forehead

and informed her he intended to talk further in the morning. She hadn't agreed, although she hadn't disagreed either. Nonetheless, he'd seen the resistance in her green eyes. It had taken the last grain of his self-control not to bring her to his chest and placate that resistance with soft assurances and numerous kisses.

First thing in the morning, he'd arrive at her realty office and check off the first part of what was keeping them apart. He had decided to visit her office on Monday anyway, although now his reasons were different.

He glanced at the clock, dreading the lengthy night awaiting him. At least there were leftovers, he mused.

He uttered a soft curse as he looked around his room. In their quick departure, he'd forgotten the leftover pizza at the restaurant.

More importantly, he'd forgotten to ask Candee why she loved beagles.

Tomorrow. There was always tomorrow. For her sake and for his, he intended to straighten out everything. Tomorrow.

~

*A*fter calling his nephew and speaking briefly to Rob, Teddy arrived at Candee's realty office at nine a.m. His arms were laden with four boxes of chocolate-covered caramels he'd bought at a local supermarket and a carryout bag from the trendy coffee house in town: two espressos topped with steamed milk, a dusting of cinnamon, and dark chocolate curls. A peace offering.

He rapped on Candee's realty door and walked in, smiling his approval at the tastefully decorated sun-lit office.

Candee sat behind an uncluttered desk with her laptop open, clicking rapidly on the keys. It appeared she'd taken extra care with her appearance, wearing a light-pink blouse and tailored black slacks. Her luxurious red hair was pulled back from her face and fastened with a floral-colored barrette, the rest of it falling to curl naturally around her shoulders.

His heart stopped. She was so beautiful.

She didn't seem quite as enraptured to see him. Her greeting consisted of a curt nod.

He held the candy toward her. "These are for you. I realize it's a little early in the morning for chocolate."

"It's never too early for chocolate." A slow smile came across her face as she stood. She accepted the candy and placed the boxes beside her laptop. "Thank you, although I can't eat all this candy."

"I can help you." Encouraged by his success, he pulled up a chair and set the coffees on her desk. "I assume you expected me, and I have four reasons for coming."

She sat back down in her chair. "Teddy, I ... The Victorian ... If you knew how much the home means to me."

"That's the main reason I'm here." An odd lump formed in his throat at her vulnerable yet unwavering expression. "I have no intention of bidding on the property anymore."

She pressed a palm to her heart. "You don't?"

"Absolutely not. Prompted by the right incentive, of course." He paused. When she didn't respond, he continued, "Besides, I certainly wouldn't want to go against you in a bidding war."

A determined glint shone in her gaze. "Considering you know I'd do anything to win?"

"Considering that fact and everything else, I won't even try. When you're bent on a course of action, I believe nothing can stop you."

"You've come to know me well in four days." She leaned back in her chair and grinned. "Besides, my twenty-thousand-dollar bid is all the money to my name, and I wouldn't have the funds to bid against you." Without warning, her grin turned into a sob.

He went around her desk and knelt, sliding his arms around her. Turning into his embrace she cried harder, murmuring between sobs about how relieved she was, and how she knew the house could be salvaged with hard work and diligence, and she planned to use the acreage for a small working farm.

When her tears waned, she stayed where she was, her head resting against his chest.

He offered a napkin from the coffee bag. "Everything better?"

Self-consciously, she dabbed at her eyes and composed her features. "I haven't allowed myself to cry in years."

"I haven't cried in a long time either," he admitted. Rising, he skimmed a kiss across her temple.

She offered a rueful grin. "What are the other reasons you're here?'

"Well, the first was to bring you coffee and chocolates, and the second was to inform you I won't be bidding on the Victorian."

"But you mentioned a 'right' incentive. What might that be?"

"I'd like a thank-you kiss in return for preferring to be your ally, not your adversary."

She smiled.

He lifted her from her chair and pulled her into his arms. Gently, he brushed his lips over hers. Her tongue swept across his lips, and he welcomed her, his body shamelessly hungry in its response. His fingers tightened possessively to draw her closer, and an eternity passed before he lifted his mouth.

"The reason you came to Roses was to find a property and

now you're giving it up," she murmured. "You would do this for me?"

He gazed into her glistening eyes, brimming with happiness.

"I would do anything for you," he answered thickly, surprised he'd spoken his thoughts aloud. "Although I truly believe the Victorian is beyond renovation."

She pulled out of his arms. "I'm a fairly good carpenter."

His gaze narrowed, although he didn't want to spoil the moment by informing her the house needed at least a dozen carpenters working around the clock—not to mention plumbers, electricians and roofers.

The silence lengthened. His heart gave a lurch at the resolve in her gaze.

"And do you know what I've learned from being a carpenter?" she asked. "Good old-fashioned perseverance and staying power. Even my simple three-inch rocking chair demanded endless hours and a lot of care."

"Making a rocking chair for a dollhouse is a lot different from tackling a five thousand square foot house that's been abandoned for years," he said.

"I'm not impatient. I'll focus on the process and—"

"I'll support you." His quiet tone stopped her from continuing. "However, from my knowledge as a contractor, sometimes you need to move on. Bringing the house up to par with city and code requirements will take a lot of capital."

Adamantly, she shook her head. "I'll never give up my dream."

He noted the guarded hope in her voice and carefully chose his words. "I have an offer for you. Your plan for after-school care is a good one, and I'd like to invest in it. Make me part of your equation." He lifted the coffees from the bag and handed her a cup. "Will you consent to viewing other properties in Roses that might also suit your dream?"

She opened her mouth, presumably to argue.

"Keep an open mind," he reminded.

"I can't accept any money from you, Teddy."

"Consider it a loan, then. I'll even throw in my free expert advice."

She managed a wan smile before sinking into her chair and thoughtfully savoring her coffee.

He glanced around the room. "Your mother owned this business?" He congratulated himself on changing their conversation's direction.

"Those were the days when my mother wasn't drinking. By the time I graduated from college, this office had been boarded up, so I earned my real estate license and opened using her name."

"Which is the reason I called you and not your competitors," he said. "I assumed you'd been in business for many years and knew the area well." Fate again, he thought.

"I wanted to continue my mother's legacy in some way. She wasn't a terrible parent, just terribly misguided." Candee absently touched her gold earrings. "And of course, the drinking and the drugs ..."

"I've noticed you wear those earrings every day. Are they from your mother?"

Sadness flickered across her beautiful face. "It's all I have left as a remembrance. She bought them at a consignment shop for my twelfth birthday. It wasn't long afterward that Desiree and I were moved to our first foster home." A hint of a smile wavered. "Now you've given me three reasons."

He grinned. She didn't miss a thing.

"I'm flying to Miami in a couple weeks to consult with Rob and see Joseph," he explained. "Joseph's a wonderful kid. I think I mentioned that on weekends, he goes to a horse training therapy facility."

"Do you have custody of your nephew?"

"Hopefully soon." Teddy exhaled a deep breath. "My brother was killed in an automobile accident a few months ago, and I should be granted guardianship of Joseph fairly soon. It's so hard for him right now ... For us ..." Teddy glanced out the window and knuckled an unexpected tear. She waited in silence while he cleared his throat before turning back to her. "I'd like you to fly down to Florida with me to meet Rob and Joseph. You alluded to a working farm for disadvantaged children and you might want to expand the concept and include animals as therapy."

"It sounds like a wonderful idea, although I can't go. I have too many commitments in Roses."

"We'll be gone from Friday afternoon until Sunday evening and you'd have almost two weeks to prepare for the trip."

"What about my real estate business?"

"Your one client is sitting across from you."

She hesitated. "I've never seen Miami."

"Bring shorts and flip-flops. You can stay at one of Rob's places. He owns apartments above several of his businesses, and one is a five-minute walk from my condo."

"I'd never impose."

"Believe me, Rob owns more properties than he knows what to do with. And didn't you advise me last evening to fly back to Miami? Well, I'm following your advice, except that I want you to join me."

CHAPTER EIGHT

*T*he next two weeks flew by in a pleasant flurry for Candee, as she and Teddy viewed prospective houses and stopped daily at the Victorian home. He'd offered advice on cost-effective strategies to modernize, while staying true to the house's character. Though they'd viewed numerous modest properties more in sync with her nonexistent budget, none came close to matching the Victorian's architectural design, aesthetics, or sheer grandeur.

Together, she and Teddy researched adding a horse farm to the property; and she'd discovered that horses, with their unique nature, were considered mirrors of a person and an excellent choice for therapy. Furthermore, being around horses bolstered a person's self-confidence, as horses were believed to relieve stress.

"You have the acreage," Teddy had encouraged her after they'd exhausted her property search.

On the last afternoon before their departure to Miami, they volunteered at the shelter. When they were about to leave, a pregnant whimpering beagle was brought in. After the veterinarian examination, it was determined the dog was approximately fifty days pregnant and due to give birth to six puppies within the week.

"Where was the dog found?" Teddy asked.

"This poor beagle was left on the side of the road." Candee gazed at the hound-dog look the beagle gave her, and her heart melted. "I may not be able to travel to Miami with you, Teddy, considering how large the beagle's stomach is. I want to be here with her when she gives birth."

He'd assured her they'd technically be gone for one day—traveling to Miami on Friday and returning to Roses on Sunday.

As he knelt beside her, she whispered, "After the beagle has her puppies, I want to keep her."

He raised his eyebrows. "Do you mean her or the puppies?"

"Both. A dog with puppies is costly for a shelter." Lightly, she caressed the dog's black and tan coat, and the dog didn't try to bite. "I'll be a foster mom until the pups can be adopted. All they need is a warm home."

"And food and nursing and a loving caregiver," he murmured, recovering admirably from his shock.

He carefully carried the compact hound dog to her own enclosure with food and water, and Candee placed a worn blanket beneath the dog.

"Try to eat, girl." She offered the beagle a piece of fruit. The dog sniffed and slowly inched toward Candee's outstretched hand.

"Beagles are known to be loving, gentle, and extremely sociable," Candee told Teddy.

Seeing his expression as he brushed a sprinkling of dog hair, which resembled black pepper, from his vest, she assured, "And beagles don't shed, except in the spring when they're ridding themselves of their winter coats."

"You know a lot about these dogs." At the sound of

Teddy's deep voice, the dog keenly watched him and wagged her tail. "Why do you love beagles so much?"

"We owned a dog once, a sweet beagle, and Desiree and I were forced to leave her behind." She hesitated, not trusting her voice to continue. "We called her 'Kisses.'"

The pregnant dog stared up at them with wide-set pleading hazel eyes.

"'Kisses.' Your dog's name was Kisses." Apparently weighing his words, Teddy carefully replied, "You're taking on a tremendous amount of work with a monstrous house filled with rubble and weeds and all these dogs."

"I cannot abandon her. And in eight weeks her pups will be adoptable. And yes, I'm naming the beagle Kisses."

She'd been ready to puff up with indignation if he'd tried to discourage her. He didn't. Instead, he smiled and offered his assistance, agreeing that Kisses was a perfect name for a beagle. Stating he wanted to "seal the Kisses decision," he pulled her close, his arms cradling her body as his lips passionately explored hers.

Hours later, Desiree joined them for a festive dinner at a new farm-to-table restaurant in downtown Roses. Although their table had ample room to accommodate the threesome comfortably, his muscled leg had touched Candee's throughout the meal. It seemed like he always made a point to keep her close to him.

Teddy had laughingly concurred with Desiree as she waved a forkful of miniature crab cake and declared, "No one in their right mind places a bid on a property that looks like a tumbledown haunted house. And now my sister is stepping up to take on a pregnant beagle about to give birth to a bunch of puppies?"

"'Kisses needs a home," Candee said staunchly. "And the children at the daycare can teach her and the puppies how to sit and stay and fetch."

"And you'll need to hire a full-time staff," Teddy said while aiming a subtle nod at Desiree. "Although knowing you, Candee, you'll attempt to juggle everything yourself."

"You've offered to help, right?"

He studied her face and replied, "Yes, and I never go back on my word."

She stared up at him, his smiling features, the firm line of his jaw, enveloped by his commanding presence. His gaze locked with hers. Both of them completely disregarded her sister's presence as he lowered his head, his lips hovering close before he kissed her lightly. Her breath caught as his bracing outdoor scent tingled her senses.

When she returned to her apartment that night, she fell into bed, pleasantly exhausted. As she did every night before retiring, she checked the bidding on the Victorian, relieved her twenty-thousand-dollar offer remained the highest.

She courted sleep, although it didn't come. She was too excited, her thoughts humming with elated expectation. Soon she would own her dream house, and she'd be building that dream with Teddy. Yes, he lived in Miami and she lived in Roses, but with Internet and phone calls and airplane travel, their relationship could continue to grow.

Her mood had lightened with each hour she'd spent with him, and life was definitely taking a turn she'd never expected. Perhaps Desiree was right and Cupid's arrow had been aimed directly at Candee and Teddy.

Sighing contentedly, she rolled onto her stomach and drifted to sleep.

CHAPTER NINE

*T*he following afternoon, Candee made sure every employee at the shelter knew to call her if Kisses went into labor. Then she and Teddy boarded the plane from Asheville, North Carolina, to Miami, Florida. The trip to the airport took less than an hour, and Teddy did the driving. Their flight was under three hours, and sudden air pockets and strong winds prompted gasps from the passengers in the cabin.

Candee was still recovering from the rough flight when an impish boy, echoing Teddy's good looks, raced to greet her and Teddy while they were retrieving their luggage at baggage claim.

"Uncle Teddy!" the boy called.

"Hey, Joseph!" Teddy squatted, fiercely hugging the boy. As he stood, he hoisted his nephew onto his shoulders.

Pivoting, he motioned to Candee. "Joseph, meet my new friend, Miss Candee Contando."

She extended her hand. "I've heard a lot about you, Joseph."

"Hi." The boy leaned over Teddy's head. "Mr. Rob said Uncle Teddy mentions you every time he calls."

"And I'm Mr. Rob." A short, heavy-set, balding man bent at the waist in an exaggerated bow. Along with a good-natured smile, his blue-eyed gaze was welcoming. He stole Candee's luggage from her and thoughtfully cocked his head. "You're too ravishing to be anyone else. Welcome to Miami, Candee."

Teddy swung Joseph back down to the floor as he offered introductions. He kept one hand possessively around her waist, and as she glanced up at him, he was staring down at her with heartfelt pride.

"No wonder she was one of your main topics when we spoke," Rob said, clapping Teddy on the back. "Everything's certainly coming up Roses, eh?"

The group dissolved into good-natured chuckling.

As they stepped out of the airport, the air of the Miami evening was balmy and inviting. Candee pulled off her paisley scarf and tucked it into her carry-on bag. Teddy walked between her and Joseph, holding their hands. As they walked to Rob's car, they passed an outdoor kiosk brimming with Valentine candy.

"No candy for me," Rob said. "I'm on a diet."

"Again?" Teddy teased.

"I haven't cheated in twenty-four hours. I'm on a roll." He kept his gaze fixed on the sidewalk and whistled an out-of-tune melody.

"We're not dieting." Teddy turned to Candee. "Carmel dark chocolate sound good?"

"I can't. My stomach is reeling from the turbulent airplane ride."

"Dark chocolate helps." He picked up two decorative gold boxes filled with candy, along with a red-foil rose and a jumbo heart swirl lollipop for Joseph.

"Chocolate and more chocolate?" she joked as he handed her the rose and boxed candy.

"Sugar and chocolate is the cure for most maladies."

"Yeah," Rob interjected. "That's been my bakery mantra for years."

She chuckled and eyed the lollipop. "You realize, Teddy, that your nephew will be on a sugar high tonight and you'll only have yourself to blame?"

"Guilty as charged." Teddy held up a hand, then swept a kiss on her lips. "I'll pick you up at Rob's apartment tomorrow at eleven."

He was so wonderfully generous, and when he kissed her, she heartily kissed him back. At least until Rob's raucous throat-clearing broke her and Teddy apart.

∼

Following a leisurely shower in Rob's high-end penthouse Saturday morning, Candee checked her appearance in the bedroom's full-length mirror. The weather was a comfortable seventy degrees, and she was pleased she'd brought a soft royal-blue crepe dress accented by gathered cropped sleeves. She rubbed a drop of her favorite rose fragrance to her wrists, and pulled on black leather ballet flats for walking ease.

She had just knotted the gold tie belt around her waist when she heard a light rap on the penthouse door. Teddy had arrived exactly at eleven a.m.

She smiled as she opened the door. Yes, he was devastatingly handsome, standing in the doorway wearing cotton khaki pants and a slim-fitting gray polo shirt that accented his strong physique. However, it was the little things that drew her to him—his kind actions, how he was true to his word, and the way his eyes lit with boyish enthusiasm whenever he described the Victorian's renovations.

"Good morning." He took her hands in his and gazed at her with bold dark eyes. "Your beauty lights up this place."

Self-consciously, she laughed. "You must be focusing on the view behind me. You know, the sixteen-foot floor-to-ceiling windows looking out onto Miami beach and 'millionaire's row.'"

He drew her to him. "No, it's you," he whispered. "Only you." His mouth came down on hers for a long passionate kiss, and her heart thumped hard in her chest.

She placed her cell phone in her handbag and slung the bag over her shoulder. Down in the lobby, they encountered a pacing Rob and an exuberant Joseph demonstrating a cartwheel across the marbled floor.

"About time, you two." Rob pointedly stared at his watch. "What normally takes me five minutes took you ten."

"We were detained," Teddy said, reclaiming Candee's hand. "Shall we all walk to your bakery?"

"Absolutely." Rob patted his round stomach. "Some of us can use the exercise."

In the glittering daylight of the promising morning, Candee tucked her fingers in the crook of Teddy's strong arm. A welcoming breeze lifted her loose hair from her shoulders like a whirlpool.

As the foursome approached Sixty-Fifth Street, Rob's body language punctuated his proud tone. "What's not to like about America's favorite vacation city?" He gestured to the glass skyscrapers on both sides of the street. "Miami boasts a trendy nightlife, boat shows, auto racing, golf, tennis, cruises and deep-sea fishing."

"And we've never done any of those activities," Teddy said dryly.

"We had a lively time on the two-night party cruise a few years back, remember?"

"Lively time?" A knowing grin crossed Teddy's face. "You were seasick the entire forty-eight hours."

They crossed an intersection, and the enticing scent from Rob's bakery beckoned them into the store like a warm embrace. Glazed donuts, masterfully iced rainbow-colored cupcakes, and towering, three-tiered layer cakes frosted with buttercream sat proudly in a row of glass cases.

"I saved your Valentine cupcake for you, Uncle Teddy," Joseph said. And I made one for Miss Candee too. We froze them, and Mr. Rob took them out of the freezer yesterday." Joseph tugged on Teddy's hand. "They're in the kitchen. Come on, I'll show you."

"Save us a table," Teddy said to Candee. "We'll be back shortly."

When half of their group had disbanded, Rob examined a display case for fingerprints while a white-aproned employee boxed an order of cinnamon buns.

Candee hung back, standing behind a parade of customers.

When Rob returned carrying two mugs of coffee and a bag of donuts, he guided her to an inviting seating area adjoining the bakery.

"Freshly baked donuts!" He exclaimed. "Twenty-four hours on a diet is long enough." He set a white bakery bag emblazoned with his Rob's Marvelous Muffins logo and the two mugs on the small round table. "Black coffee, right?"

"Thank you." She inhaled the mouth-watering scent of chocolate iced donuts rolled in sprinkles and the aroma of rich dark coffee. "Your hospitality is generous, and both your places—the penthouse and this bakery—are amazing."

"I don't have any complaints about flattery." He took a large swallow of his coffee. "Keep it coming."

"I'd gain ten pounds in a week if I worked here." She grinned. "A bakery like yours in my hometown would be well-received."

He flashed a smile. "I own a half dozen bakeries in Miami. I haven't considered opening out-of-state, although you never know."

Rob went on to describe the process of running a bakery, embroidering his account of the time he'd changed a hit recipe and used confectioners' sugar instead of granulated, which had resulted in a string of complaints.

Her turquoise and silver bracelets cheerfully clinked against her coffee mug as she drank and listened. He was such a genial man and so talkative, she could imagine him having a conversation without her, chatting non-stop to an empty chair.

"Enough about me." His telescope gaze gave her a measured look. "Let's talk about your grand plans for the Victorian, Candee."

"Hasn't Teddy told you?"

He nodded confirmation. "Now I want to hear it from you."

She blew out an audible breath. "To begin with, every bathroom requires a complete gut job, and the carpeting in each room needs to be pulled up." She paused. "The wood floors are trashed, and Teddy recommended restoring them using four-inch red-oak planks."

"Do you have funds to pay for all these renovations?" Rob flatly asked.

His tone didn't intimidate her in the least. "No. I'll take out loans."

"And how do you intend to pay back these loans? All these restorations will take endless capital."

She let the reality of his words hang in the air between them. She'd learned to stay quiet when she wasn't certain how to answer, and she needed to think before replying. Her foster background, dealing with different people's expectations, had taught her that.

"I'll work extra hours at the hardware store," she said. "And I can wield tools and ladders. There's nothing like carpentry to test a person's patience."

Mentally, she thanked her "forever" foster father for permitting her to work with him in his woodshop.

She met Rob's piercing blue gaze and waved a dismissive hand at herself. "Who knows? Maybe I'll even sell a house or two in the meantime."

"Teddy said your perseverance and goals are admirable."

"I'm going to be the type of caregiver who attends every child's basketball game, every concert ..." She forced herself to keep her tone calm and unemotional. "These disadvantaged kids need support."

"I've invested in Teddy's ventures for years, and he's never let me down. He approves of your project and he oversees numerous home-improvement crews."

"We'll give it our best shot."

"The hallmark of a successful baker is self-discipline, and the same goes for real estate." Rob gave a big throaty laugh. "At first, Teddy wanted to raze the house and build low-income housing on the five-acre lot. Our business ethos is to give to those less fortunate."

In the space of seconds, Teddy's ideas collided with hers, and she could see the merit in his plans for the property.

"He never told me," she softly replied.

"You're the best thing that's happened to him in a long time. Has he mentioned his childhood to you?"

She swallowed a deep drink of the exquisitely brewed coffee. "Hardly anything."

"I encouraged him to show you his old homestead," Rob said. "He said he's too embarrassed."

"It can't be any worse than my childhood homes."

Instantly, she was ambushed by scenes from her adolescence. Whenever her birthday had come around, she had waited, hoping for a birthday cake. The cake never came. Neither did the candles, or the balloons, or the birthday gifts.

"Teddy came from nothing," Rob said, "and he and his brother were constantly beaten by his drunken father. When life gets punched out of you, only the outstanding persevere. Unfortunately, after a hard childhood, a person's trust no longer comes easy."

She confirmed his words with a sad smile. Despite his outward bravado, Rob had an astute understanding of people.

"And what about your foster families?" he asked.

She shrugged. "Nothing to say."

He propped his elbows on the table, the gleam in his eyes matching his shiny round face. "Up until now, Teddy's been a confirmed bachelor like me. I'm the furthest a person can get from being a wedding expert, but he genuinely cares about you. He can't stop looking at you whenever you're together."

She stifled a denial as a giggling four-year-old boy raced to the table with Teddy close behind.

"We're back, Miss Candee," Joseph announced. "And we brought your Valentine surprise cupcake." He held up a basket, revealing a red muffin set on a red doily. Piped white icing gel on the muffin read, "Life is butter with you."

Her lips twitched with a grin. Impulsively, she hugged the adorable boy. "Thank you." She turned to Rob. "Clever sentiment, Rob."

Rob laughed. "They're all different. Took me weeks to come up with appropriate Valentine adages that wouldn't offend any customers."

"Taste the muffin and tell me what the surprise is, Miss Candee," Joseph said. "I'll give you a hint. It has something do with kisses."

"Joseph, you're not supposed to give any hints to Candee, remember?" Teddy hooked his hands in his front pockets. His slow, devastating smile eclipsed all the busyness of the bustling bakery. "It's a taste test and she's supposed to discover the surprise by herself."

Candee bit into the muffin and briefly closed her eyes. The combination of strawberries and butter was delicious. She washed down the muffin with coffee, then took another bite. "There's chocolate inside. Wait ..." she continued around a mouthful of cupcake. "A candy kiss is in the middle?"

"You guessed the surprise!" Joseph jumped up and down. "Like it?"

She laughed. "I love it."

"Me too." Teddy kissed her forehead, then pulled up a wing chair and sat facing her.

"Where's *your* Valentine muffin?" she teased.

"Gone in three bites."

"What was on yours?"

"The Browning quote." He kept his gaze on hers. "'Grow old along with me. The best is yet to be.'"

Positively emanating good cheer, Rob said, "And they all lived long and happily ever after. Long because it was for forty years, and happy for ... two months."

Teddy grinned, glanced at his watch, then back at Candee. "Later today I want to take you to Joseph's horse ranch so you can see him ride his pony."

"I'm looking forward to it."

The cell phone in her purse rang. She pulled out her phone and checked the caller ID. "Please excuse me." She held up an index finger and answered the call.

When she clicked off, she took several quick breaths. Her gaze flitted to the threesome staring at her before settling on Teddy. "It was one of the volunteers at the shelter. My beagle has gone into labor."

"Kisses?" Teddy's eyebrows drew together. "Don't labors take a long time?"

"For a beagle, anywhere from six to eighteen hours." She matched his stare with a firm one of her own. "I'm sorry. I have to leave this afternoon."

Teddy pressed his lips together and offered a weak smile. "I know how much this beagle means to you." He took his phone from his pocket and began checking the Internet. "There's a direct fight to Asheville leaving at four o'clock and one seat is available."

"Will you book it for me? I'll text Desiree and ask her if she can pick me up at the airport."

After the reservation was made, Teddy set his phone on the table. "Done. I'll keep my return flight to Roses on Sunday night so I can spend more time with Joseph."

"Yes, of course." Looking at the boy, she said, "I'm sorry I can't see you ride your pony."

"That's okay, Miss Candee," Joseph replied. "I ride him every weekend. I love horses! I love every animal in the world!"

She laughed. "Animals and children are very special."

Teddy stroked the auburn curls falling about her shoulders. "You're not even gone yet, and I miss you."

"Okay you two flames, save it for later." Rob cut his gaze to Teddy. Giving him a meaningful look, he lowered his tone. "Your lawyer called this morning. He couldn't reach you and left a message with me. It's about a court date to finalize your guardianship." Rob raised his tone, apparently for Joseph's benefit, who'd been intently watching them. "Hey Teddy, can I talk to you in the back?"

"Sure." Teddy quickly stood. "I wanted to behold the new commercial mixer you purchased for the kitchen, anyway."

"The heavy-duty one? It broke. The grinder lasted a week."

Teddy gave a sharp laugh. "Aren't you glad you came to Miami to meet the special people in my life?" he asked Candee.

She smiled. "Very glad."

He glided his knuckles down her cheek. "Is it all right if I leave Joseph with you for a few minutes?"

"My absolute pleasure."

Teddy grabbed an activity sheet and crayons at the counter and placed them on the table for his nephew. "How about sketching me a horse, buddy?"

"I want to draw the pony I ride at the ranch. His name is Blackjack because he's black."

Candee swallowed a chuckle as the men headed to the kitchen.

"What an excellent name for a pony," she said to Joseph. "I'm sure Blackjack is a beauty." She sat back in her chair, sipping her coffee and watching Joseph color. When Teddy's phone vibrated, she automatically picked it up and scanned the displayed number.

"You can answer it," Joseph said. "Uncle Teddy doesn't mind. I answer his phone all the time."

She debated. The phone number was identified by two initials—YE. A business call, she wondered? Assuming the call might be important, she answered. "Hello?"

"Who's this?" a woman asked.

Candee frowned into the phone. "Candee Contando. And you?"

"Yvonne Evette. Is this Teddy's phone?"

"Yes. May I take a message?"

"Put Teddy on the line," the woman said.

"He's not here."

"Tell him I'll be in Madrid another week and to phone me as soon as he gets this message. That means immediately." The woman hung up.

Candee stared at his phone as she set it on the table. "Who's Yvonne Evette?" she asked aloud, not expecting an answer.

"You mean Miss Yvonne?" Joseph made a face. "She's Uncle Teddy's other girlfriend and she's famous. We watch her on TV."

The shock of Teddy's betrayal knocked the air from Candee's lungs. She swallowed hard.

Unfortunately, Teddy and Rob chose that moment to emerge from the kitchen. They were obviously enjoying themselves, laughing and talking. Rob veered off to speak with an employee. Teddy was still grinning when he approached Candee's table.

He stopped, his probing gaze fixing on her. "What's wrong? You've gone pale."

She pushed back her chair. "Your cell phone rang and I answered it. I shouldn't have—I thought it might be important."

"Who was it?"

"A call from Spain."

Teddy stiffened. "Yvonne?"

"Yes, and she said to call her immediately."

Unnoticed, Rob strolled to the table. "Anything wrong?"

Heartsick from sadness and fury and defeat, Candee shivered and rubbed her arms. "Rob, where's the restroom?"

He pointed to a sign, and she shot past him.

"Candee, wait." Teddy strode purposefully after her. "I can explain."

She inhaled a tortured breath. She'd heard enough explanations from her ex to last a lifetime. And she'd never allow Teddy to see how much his duplicity had hurt her.

"It's not what it seems." He caught her wrist, and she snapped around. "Look," he said, "I've been seeing Yvonne for several months. She travels a lot and I ... I don't do long-distance relationships well."

Tears sprang to Candee's eyes. Firmly, determinedly, she held them back. "You don't do any relationship well."

"Please let me explain."

She deliberately stared down at his hand until he released her.

"I'll walk back to the penthouse and call a taxi to the airport," she said. "Please don't follow me. And tell Rob thank you for everything. Kiss Joseph good-bye for me and tell him I love animals too." She pivoted and entered the restroom. Inside, she splashed cold water on her face and peered at her reflection in the mirror above the sink. Her pallid complexion emphasized her emerald-green eyes, giving her a much-too-vulnerable appearance.

Again she was a fool, and she only had herself to blame. How could she have believed it was possible to fall in love with a man after knowing him a few short weeks?

Love. Love happened to other people, not to her. The sooner she came to grips with reality, the simpler her life would become. No more broken hearts, she vowed. Not ever again.

Two hours later she stood alone in the Miami airport, waiting for the boarding to begin.

To pass the time while waiting in line, she checked the foreclosure website. She gasped, almost dropping her phone when the house came on the screen. Her bid was no longer the highest.

She refreshed her phone. Surely, there must be a mistake.

No. The new bid was $40,000, driving the next bid to $60,000—money she didn't have.

This couldn't be happening. Her stomach felt heavy, her heartbeat raced.

Quickly, she texted Desiree. *I logged online at the airport, and the Victorian is now at 40K. Who bid on MY house?*

Online means the Internet, came Desiree's reply. *So that means anyone on the world-wide web. No use worrying. Whatever happened, we'll sort it when u get home. Have a safe flight and see u in Asheville.*

Candee attempted to pull her mind away from one looming fear. She might lose the house.

Another text floated across her screen, this one from Teddy. *Have u boarded the plane?*

He'd texted numerous times since she'd abruptly left Rob's bakery, and she'd ignored him.

However, he'd made and paid for her plane reservation and she knew she should text him.

Soon, she replied.

Can I call you tomorrow?

She hesitated. Her cold, clammy hands clutched the phone tighter.

Something prompted her to ask, although surely his answer would be no.

Did you place a bid on the Victorian house? she texted.

Air stopped entering her lungs as she waited for his response. Time seemed to be slowing down until a single word appeared on her phone.

Yes.

*a*s usual, Desiree had arrived at the country club before Candee. Candee hung her fur capelet by the door and greeted her sister with a hug.

Desiree looked gorgeous in a red velvet figure-hugging pant suit. She went back to arranging a plate of chocolate-covered strawberries on a silver serving tray. The club was empty, save for black-suited waiters setting glass vases of red tulips and rose peonies on every table.

Candee appraised her own outfit—a sleeveless petal-pink lace dress. Unlined along the hem, the dress allowed a peek-aboo of her long legs. She'd parted her hair on the side and let the thick curls flow down the opposite shoulder.

Satisfied with the strawberry arrangement, Desiree turned to her. "Finally, I was able to talk you into attending the dinner dance. You can leave those puppies alone for a few hours. Valentine's Day is one of the biggest events at the club. Thanks for coming early to help me finish decorating."

"You insisted you needed help, although there's so much to admire." Candee looked around the room. "The lace ribbons and pom-pom wreaths are glittery and sophisticated, and those smooch balloons are gorgeous."

"White balloons with a stamp of my red lipstick." Desiree puckered her glistening red lips.

Candee smiled and fingered an arrow-toting Cupid on the banquet table. "No use in me sitting in my apartment with Kisses and her six puppies, watching television and hoping that Meg Ryan and Tom Hanks will get me through the evening."

"Her puppies are adorable. So firm and plump."

"And active," Candee replied. "Plus, they've doubled their weight in less than two weeks. Kisses is the best mom in the world. I supply high-quality puppy food and a vitamin mineral tablet, and she does the rest."

Desiree popped a chocolate-covered strawberry into her mouth and smiled. "All is well then."

Was it? The lump in Candee's throat threatened to choke her, and tears burned her eyelids. She swallowed and poured herself a glass of water. She wouldn't cry. She was strong and had made a vow to herself.

Desiree was watching her closely. "Have you heard from Teddy?"

"He's texted me every day and apologized numerous times about Yvonne, although it doesn't matter anymore." Candee forced herself to sound calm and detached. "As far as I know, he hasn't returned to Roses. He said something about being tied up in Miami court because of Joseph's guardianship."

"Did you text him back?"

"Only to tell him I landed safely." She missed him intensely, especially on a night like tonight, Valentine's Day. She squeezed her eyes shut, remembering the feel of his strong calloused hand around her waist while they'd danced, his lips capturing hers.

"If I was that guy with the same first and last names," he'd said. "I'd have rented a snowplow to meet you at the country club tonight."

How could he have become so important to her in the short time they'd known each other? Each day that passed, she felt more and more empty without him. She'd even been tempted to answer his texts with an invitation to join her for dinner at Tony's. That night they'd gone there, he'd said that, like her, Italian food was his favorite in all the world.

But Teddy lived in Miami with Yvonne, and Candee lived in Roses with Kisses and her puppies.

Once she allowed them in, her tormenting memories took over. She'd loved listening to his remodeling ideas, the quiet decisiveness in his voice when they'd agreed that horse therapy suited her project perfectly. And then there'd been the comforting reassurance of knowing they were venturing into these daunting tasks side by side.

Hah! Had he played her for a fool the entire time, planning to take her house right out from under her? The auction had just closed, and most likely demolition would begin any day. Candee promised herself she'd never drive down Thompson Lane again. Idly, she wondered if Teddy would manage the project himself, or send one of his many home-improvement crews to demolish the house.

Desiree had advised her to set her sights elsewhere. Perhaps a five-hundred-foot Cape Cod made more sense, considering her budget. Smaller dreams were more realistic.

She opened her eyes.

Her sister's gaze clouded with concern and she clasped Candee's hands. "You know, we tried to raise the funds, but neither Scott nor I had an extra $40,000 hidden under our pillowcases."

"Thank you." Not only was Desiree her sister, but she was also a true friend.

After that, Desiree adeptly changed the subject, resulting

in a half hour of setting red candles around the room. But Candee's fragile composure began to slip. Other guests would be arriving soon, and she wasn't sure she could make conversation with anyone. She attempted to bolster herself by remembering she'd agreed to attend the event for only two hours. She eyed an ornate grandfather clock on the opposite wall. An hour and a half left.

Desiree jumped to her feet as two men entered the room. "Scott is here, and he brought ... Allen Allen?" she shrieked. Desiree turned so pale, Candee feared the many chocolate-covered strawberries Desiree had eaten had made her ill.

"You're joking, right?" Candee said to her sister. "You invited him?"

Desiree seemed rooted to the floor. "No, actually, I didn't."

Candee threw up her hands. "I'm leaving by seven o'clock," she reminded Desiree.

"Dinner is served at six, leaving you plenty of time." Desiree's gaze narrowed on Scott. Then she grabbed Candee's hand and started toward the two well-dressed men for introductions.

Dusk was streaking pomegranate colors in the darkening sky when Allen seated Candee to his right for dinner. A waiter set glasses of sparkling apple and pear cider at each place setting.

Teddy preferred coffee, she thought, reminding herself that she should be indifferent to his choice of beverage. She frowned. She didn't feel indifferent to anything about him. She missed the bantering they'd shared, the warm strength of his strong muscled body close to hers.

"The first course is a cheese and hazelnut green salad," Desiree declared to the others at the table, rousing Candee from her thoughts of Teddy. "For the entrée, the club is serving chicken in champagne sauce."

"I'm certain the meal will be delicious," Candee replied graciously. She took a long swallow of cider and lapsed into a reflective silence.

~

*H*olding his nephew's hand, Teddy strode into the Roses country club exactly at six o'clock. The flight from Miami to Asheville had been bumpy, and getting his truck from the long-term rental parking lot had taken longer than he'd planned. The Valentine's Day festivities were well underway. A quick assessment of his worn jeans, polo shirt, and vest assured him he was underdressed for the formal occasion.

"Uncle Teddy, where is Miss Candee?" Joseph hopped on one foot. "Look—they have candy hearts in those little glasses by the window. Can I get some?"

Before Teddy could reply, the boy had scurried off. He gazed at him—a bundle of boundless energy and perfection, his dark eyes framed by thick black lashes. His adorable nephew, now his son to raise to the best of his ability.

I can do this, Christian, Teddy thought. Two weeks of endless paperwork had resulted in Teddy being awarded legal guardianship of Joseph.

It had been a difficult two weeks. After Candee had left Miami so abruptly, Teddy had tasted a painful defeat. No matter how much he plunged into his work, or cared for Joseph, or signed papers in the courtroom, he couldn't fully concentrate.

And then he'd made his decision.

His mind told him to stay in Miami. His heart told him otherwise.

"Are you expecting dinner guests?" he'd asked her that night when they'd danced.

Her beautiful green eyes had stared into his. "Not unless they're bringing chocolate," *she'd quipped.*

She possessed such enthusiasm, such spirit. And he'd hurt her by not being upfront about his relationship with Yvonne. Although in all fairness, he hadn't considered Yvonne a part of his life after he'd met Candee.

"Uncle Teddy! There she is!" Joseph shouted around a mouthful of pink candy hearts.

Teddy's gaze riveted on Candee. She sat at an elegantly decorated table with Desiree and two men. Teddy recognized Scott from the night he'd seen him at the country club. But the other man? He'd better not be that guy with two first names.

He grabbed Joseph's hand and stalked past a group of waiters serving champagne in fluted glasses to the guests.

He stopped Joseph from grabbing a white balloon, and he let a waiter show Joseph where the balloons were stored in an adjoining room.

When he looked at Candee again, she was out of her chair walking toward him.

"Teddy?"

She was exquisite, a glamorous, stunning goddess. Her glossy auburn hair hung to the side, a rosy tint creeping up her flawless cheeks. Her lacy pink dress displayed her alluring figure to full advantage. He was so relieved. Desiree had responded to his texts and told him that she'd finally persuaded Candee to attend this dinner.

He took her hands in his. "You are gorgeous."

She grinned shyly. "Thank you."

His gaze wandered across the crowded dining room, and he was annoyed at their lack of privacy, for all he wanted to do was kiss her inviting lips. Already, the hum of conversation was fading, and several diners were staring at them.

He slipped his arm around her shoulders and guided her into the hallway.

"Why are you here?" she asked.

"Because I missed you."

Her green eyes were soft and tender. "I missed you too."

"Can you leave?" He gestured impatiently around the corner, indicating the threesome at Candee's table.

"Yes, of course. I'll get my capelet."

"Hi, Miss Candee!" Joseph skipped over to them holding three white balloons. "Did you know Uncle Teddy and I flew all the way from Miami today?"

"Joseph, I'm thrilled you're here." Candee affectionately embraced the little boy.

"Uncle Teddy said today is Valentine's Day. I like balloons," Joseph said.

"We've noticed." Chuckling, Teddy put an arm around Candee's waist and held Joseph's hand in the other. He glanced toward the dining room, grinning when he noted Desiree's thumbs-up and conspiratorial smile.

"Where are we going?" Candee asked as they exited the club. Teddy buckled Joseph into the child car seat, then came around and opened the door for her.

"I want to show you the Valentine's gift I bought you." He started the car, and they covered the miles to Thompson Lane in under fifteen minutes.

"I'm still eating the chocolate from two weeks ago," Candee said. She tackled a white balloon that had floated into the front seat and turned to give it back to Joseph. When she turned to face front again, she paled, "Please, Teddy, don't drive down this road."

"How else can you see your Valentine's gift?"

He parked in front of the Victorian, then went around to unbuckle Joseph. The boy raced to the tire swing, leaving three forgotten white balloons in the car.

Coming swiftly to the passenger side, Teddy opened Candee's door.

In the deepening dusk, she followed his gaze to the large red SOLD sign posted on the front door.

"Congratulations," she said softly.

"The Victorian isn't mine. It's yours."

She flashed him a dubious look, then gazed blindly ahead. "I don't understand."

"Some men buy roses for Valentine's Day, some buy candy. I prefer to buy houses." He paused, continuing in a solemn voice. "And this particular house is for you."

"Me?" She sucked in a breath and her eyes widened. She stared at the house with the same wistfulness he'd seen on her face the first day they'd met.

"Teddy—I ... I can't possibly accept such a gift."

"Yes, you can, under one condition."

"And that is?"

"You allow me to help you renovate."

"How? You're in Miami."

He heard the pain in her voice, and his heart squeezed.

"Not anymore. I'm selling my apartment and moving to Roses, although my realty business will require that I fly to Miami a couple of times a month." He framed her lovely face between his hands and gazed into her shining green eyes. "I'm assuming you'll let Joseph and me adopt one of the beagle pups."

"You can adopt all six," she gladly agreed. Leaning back, she stared lovingly at him. "Will you please tell me the reason you bid against me?"

"I'd intended to bid all along, and your sister knew my plan. Somehow along the way, I managed to mess things up. I never meant to hurt you, and I'm sorry."

She glided her fingers through his hair. "You texted your apology a great many times and you're forgiven." She paused, glancing at the tumbledown Victorian and Joseph skipping up and down the porch steps. "Where will you and your nephew live?"

"I didn't want to stop at one house when I could buy two." Chuckling, Teddy gestured to Mr. Dunworthy's home. "He was more than happy to sell, and he'll be moving into a retirement community so he can be closer to his son."

"You're doing all this for me? Why?"

He hugged her close, breathing in her shiny hair, the scent of sweet and spicy roses.

"Because building a new life often begins with tearing down a few walls." He smiled at the stunning woman nestled in his arms. "Candee Contando, I love you."

"I love you too," she whispered.

And then he kissed her, sealing the most important deal of his life.

THE END

A NOTE FROM JOSIE

Dear Friend,

House flipping captured my imagination long before I wrote a single word of this story. I've spent countless hours watching home-improvement television shows, marveling at how a crumbling building transforms into a place of warmth and beauty. That image was the perfect backdrop for a love story.

I hope Cupid and Roses, North Carolina, have found a small corner of your heart.

If you loved this sweet romance, please help other readers discover *1-800-CUPID* by posting your review. Reviews make an enormous difference for independent authors, and I am grateful for every single one.

The series continues with:

• *1-800-CHRISTMAS*— a holiday romance set in Roses, with a sneak peek chapter included at the end of this book

• *1-800-IRELAND* — Kathleen, from *Oh Danny Boy*, finally gets her own happily-ever-after, alongside Rob, a reader favorite from this series.

- *1-800-SUMMER*— Andrew, a Scottish hero, and Belle, a woman who loves horses.
- *1-800-NEW YEAR*— Lincoln and Shanice's story.
- *Christmas in the Air*— a sweet holiday romance about a single mother, her son, and the new pediatrician in town.

1-800-CUPID is available in ebook, Paperback, Large Print Paperback, Hardcover, and Audiobook.

Before I go, I want to leave you with this: I started writing because I was afraid not to. The dream mattered too much to walk away from. Whatever it is you've been putting off, the plan you keep revisiting, the door you haven't opened, take the chance. Do what you love.

My Spotify Play List for 1-800-CUPID is here.

With sincere appreciation for your support,

Josie Riviera

Want more sweet Valentine romances?
1-800-CUPID
A Valentine To Cherish
I Love You More
A Chocolate-Box Valentine
Valentine Hearts

Want more of the 1-800-Series, Flipping For You?
Click here.

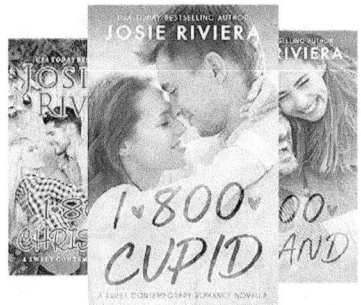

Or grab the 1-800-Series Collection.

The entire series! 6 sweet romances in 1 giant boxed set.

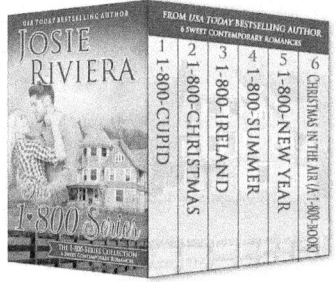

5 STAR READER REVIEWS

InD'Tale Magazine Review:

"Candee Contando and Teddy Winchester both want to purchase an old Victorian home on 5 acres at a rock-bottom price. Candee wants to refurbish the home and use it as a safe haven for kids who don't have a home. She and her sister spent their teenage years in foster homes, so she wants to help others in the same situation. Teddy wants to tear it down, split up the acreage, and put low-budget homes on the land to turn a quick profit. He recently became the guardian to his young nephew after his brother died, leaving Joseph an orphan. He needs cash to pay medical bills and lawyers' fees regarding Joseph's guardianship.

This is a novella. The author does a good job of creating the story environment and giving credence to the conflict between Teddy and Candee.

This is a sweet story and these characters are all likable. This is a pleasant story that is safe for teens and adults."

5 star Reader Reviews:

"Both Candee and Teddy want to buy the same old, dilapidated Victorian house. While Candee wants to remodel it and use it as a recreational facility for handicapped children, Teddy wants to use it as investment, destroy the residence, and build several small houses on the huge land. Although their goals should oppose them, attraction sizzles between them.

I enjoyed reading this sweet story, well-written, relaxing, and easy to read and will look forward to the other books in the series." - Amazon Reviewer

"This is a wonderful heart warming romance set in the small town of Rose. The characters are well developed and likeable. You want them to get together. They storyline flows well and the writing is engaging. I enjoyed this novella very much." - Amazon Reviewer

RECIPE FOR ROB'S SURPRISE MUFFINS

Makes: 12 muffins

Ingredients:

6 tablespoons butter

3/4 cup sugar

2 eggs

1/2 cup milk

14 strawberries, fresh or defrosted frozen

red food coloring

2 cups all-purpose flour

1/4 teaspoon salt

1 tablespoon baking powder

Hershey's Kisses, Hugs or strawberry jam

Directions:

Preheat the oven to 350 degrees Fahrenheit.

In a large bowl, cream butter and sugar. Mix eggs one at a time and add milk.

Rinse strawberries and mash. Stir berries into the butter and milk mixture, adding a few drops of red liquid food coloring.

In separate bowl, sift flour, salt and baking powder, and stir. Add flour mixture to the berry mixture and stir with a wooden spoon until the white disappears.

Line muffin tins with paper liners. Drop the batter from a tablespoon to fill the cups halfway. If you are adding the "surprise", place an unwrapped Kiss, Hug or 1/2 teaspoon of jam in the middle of each muffin. Then spoon batter to fill almost to the top.

Bake until muffins begin to brown and a toothpick inserted

near the center (but not in the Kiss) comes out clean, approximately 20 to 25 minutes.

Remove muffins from tin. Cool. Serve warm in a basket lined with red doilies.

Desiree Contando had gained weight. Not a lot, although the extra ten pounds on her five-foot-four-inch frame were enough to make her favorite linen skirt fit snugly around her waist. When she was stressed, she ate pumpkin pie. Lately, she'd eaten a lot of pumpkin pie, and she had blamed it on Thanksgiving.

However, it was more than the delicious turkey dinner her sister, Candee, had served. The cause of Desiree's stress was the rundown Queen-Anne style home she'd purchased that morning.

"Your house is beautiful." Candee's voice came from behind her. "Now we both live on Thompson Lane!"

Desiree swallowed hard. "Maybe my house will be beautiful in a thousand years."

She shouldn't have done this. She should have dashed out of the lawyer's office as soon as the closing papers had been handed over for her to sign.

"Mr. Dunworthy, the former owner, never got around to updating the home, and then Teddy didn't have time," Candee said. "Your house won't take long to restore. My dilapidated Victorian is proof that even the most ramshackle house can be renovated."

Teddy and Candee had met in Roses, North Carolina, when Teddy came from Miami searching for a house to flip. They'd married, and together with Teddy's nephew, Joseph, they'd moved into a sprawling Victorian. Teddy had been granted legal guardianship of Joseph a few months earlier.

Desiree pushed out a tight breath. "Your Victorian still needs tons of work."

"Thankfully, it has come a long way." Candee stepped to Desiree's side and flitted her a once-over. She carried a box of pumpkin muffins. "A housewarming token," she'd declared, with a promise of something better coming on Christmas Eve.

"You've accomplished so much this year," Desiree said.

"I'm following your example. Advocating justice for low-income families and children is a daunting task. Fortunately, you're a talented attorney."

"I'm just doing the best job I can."

"You're ensuring the poorest people receive fairness. I respect you." Candee's gaze wandered to the rambling house. "You have more than enough acreage on your property for horses."

"I'll leave horses to your animal expertise. And puppies."

Months earlier, Candee had adopted Kisses, a pregnant beagle, from the local animal shelter. Of the six puppies Kisses had birthed, only one remained, as Candee had sold the rest.

Candee's emerald eyes glowed. "Boomer is adorable—all black and white and tan. And he loves to eat."

"Are you planning to sell him?"

"He'd make a great companion for a special someone."

"I'm sure you'll find a forever home for him."

"I'm sure I will." Candee smirked. "Speaking of animals, Teddy finished the stable for Joseph's horse therapy. He converted a large shed, and Joseph loves the Haflinger horse. I did my research and the horse is small, with a calm temperament."

"You're wonderful parents. I'm thrilled for all of you." Desiree stared at her house. It seemed to stare back, taunting her. She took a slight step and pressed her lips together. "I don't know if I can do this."

"Of course you can. You're experiencing buyer's remorse." Candee gave Desiree's hand a gentle squeeze. "Everyone panics after buying their first house. Remember, Teddy and I are only two doors away. If you need anything, text me. Better yet, flag me from your driveway."

"Please thank Teddy for selling the house to me at such a bargain price. I'd never have been able to find such a terrific value on my own." Desiree attempted animation, and knew she wavered.

"You have a successful job, and now a home to call your

own." Candee kept her hand on Desiree's. "Look how far you've come."

"We," Desiree corrected, keeping her voice light. If she began reminiscing about their miserable childhood, she'd lose it. If she shared her thoughts, they'd both lose it.

The women had been shuffled to five different foster homes in their teens after the state had deemed their parents unfit. Drugs and drink were only part of the issue, as their parents had also struggled with mental health problems. They had died a short time after landing in jail.

Candee broke the somber mood with an encouraging beam. "Just think, you'll pay off the mortgage in thirty years."

"Thirty years." Desiree groaned. "It'll take me forever to find someone with the expertise to fix this house on my limited budget." She paused, willing herself to say her ex-boyfriend's name aloud. "Scott had promised to help."

Not physically, of course, because Scott never got his hands dirty. Nonetheless, he'd agreed to rent the dormer apartment in her attic. In addition, he'd referred his handyman cousin to tackle the house repairs at a reasonable cost.

Some boyfriend. Some *ex*. Desiree had counted on the rental income to help pay her mortgage, and a jack-of-all-trades guy to get the job done. Finally, she had her own house, but no one to share it with. No happily-ever-after.

"Scott is in the past. Forget him," Candee said. "What's worse than a guy who is only around during the good times?"

"I know. It's just . . ."

It was just that it seemed like years had passed since her and Scott's argument, although the breakup had occurred the previous evening when he'd accompanied her to the final walk-through of the house.

"Are you joking? This tumble-down nightmare is your new house?" he'd shouted.

"Well, if you had taken time out of your day before now to see it, you wouldn't be shocked," Desiree had replied. "The owner was elderly, and I told you the house needed a facelift."

"A facelift?" Scott had laughed. "Wow, Desiree. The house is a disaster. Is that your smooth-talking attorney jargon kicking into gear?"

"Are you ready to go inside?" Candee asked.

Desiree shifted and checked her shoulder bag for the house key.

Nope. She didn't have it.

"It's better Scott exited before you made a serious commitment to each other." Candee shuffled forward. "Besides, small-town life didn't fit his high-profile aspirations."

"True."

In Roses, life was slower, and people were friendly. A bandstand featured hometown entertainment. Tony's, the local pizzeria, had been there forever. Quaint and charming, the town hadn't given much thought to modernizing.

And now that Thanksgiving was over, the small town was transformed into a magical Christmas wonderland, a virtual postcard. Soon, snow would dust the pine tree branches and outlying mountaintops with a white sheen. Horse-drawn carriages circled the village green every weekend, and scents of gingerbread and cinnamon courtesy of local artisans filled the air. A holiday baking contest was held every year, and Desiree always entered her pistachio cake. She'd never won, although the twenty-five-dollar entry fee was donated to the local animal shelter.

Certainly, the happy Yuletide season and sense of community were reasons Desiree loved Roses and never wanted to leave.

A gust of icy air swept across the house's expansive front lawn, causing the oak tree branches to sway. The chilliness was a firm reminder that winter would soon secure a foothold on their Blue Ridge Mountain town. The wind was like a physical nudge, blowing across Desiree's thin navy suit jacket and bare legs.

She gripped the blue headband holding her thick blond hair in place.

She was out of luck. Her hair had blown into a mass of unmanageable waves.

Willing herself forward, Desiree stared at the various-shaped slate shingles on the roof necessitating repair, and the patterns of varicolored brick laying up the exterior walls. A century ago, the house had been designed to impress. Regardless, did anyone else use green, red, black, blue, and beige on one house?

She shouldered her red tote bag and matched Candee's steps.

This was a moment that Desiree had envisioned sharing with Scott. A life-changing threshold, embarking on their future together. They'd discuss her vision for the house, spend cozy winter evenings thumbing through decorating magazines, and wander paint stores discussing the perfect shade of dove white.

Velvet red ribbons and vibrant green garlands decorating the home's enormous rooms would celebrate Christmas in department-store style, and glittery white lights strung across the expansive front porch would create festive charm.

Now, all these special yet-to-be created memories would be done without Scott, because he was gone.

Her chest tightened, and she told herself to rein in her disappointment. Quietly to herself, she'd even hoped he'd pop the marriage question, bringing their dating arrangement to a happy-ending conclusion. She'd become Mrs. Scott Black, who lived in the beautiful Queen-Anne home on Thompson Lane.

Wow, had she ever been living in a fantasy world.

Between yesterday and today, the dream had disintegrated, and marriage was no longer in the cards. She was reaching thirty years old and every romantic relationship had resulted in a bad breakup. She was beginning to think she would forever be single and relegated to being addressed as Miss Desiree Contando.

Candee was staring at her, apparently wondering about Desiree's peculiar behavior, and why it was taking her so long to enter her new home.

"Desiree?" Candee tucked a strand of auburn hair beneath her faded baseball cap. "I know you're worried about taking on the house repairs, and I understand. When I mentioned to Teddy about your split with Scott, he made inquiries and found a carpenter for you. The guy's relocating here from Atlanta, Georgia. Apparently, Roses is his hometown. He told Teddy he'd like to give back to the community."

"Why would he leave Atlanta with the holidays a few weeks away?" Desiree asked. "Does his family live in the area?"

"Teddy didn't mention anything."

"And this guy's willing to start giving back by renovating my house?" With an overall sweep of her hands, Desiree gestured to the overgrown lawn, the neglected front porch, the weathered slate shingles on the steeply pitched roof.

"Yes. Teddy talked with him, and the guy will be arriving today."

"Does he know how much work my house demands?" Desiree challenged.

"You'll have to ask him yourself. He's reported to be talented and honest."

"Let's hope he's also cheap."

"He'll give you a good price." Candee firmly grasped Desiree's elbow, guiding her up the gravel driveway. "Teddy wanted to make amends for selling you this house when you clearly have reservations. He knows you're in a bind now with Scott gone."

Right. An understatement, to say the least.

Desiree changed her focus from her home's corner tower to Candee. "Who is this carpenter?"

"Keiran O'Malley."

Keiran O'Malley.

His name lodged in her throat. She had to fight down the feelings stirring within her.

"The O'Malleys owned O'Malley's Irish pub, which shut down many years ago," she managed to say.

The image of a tall, green-eyed guy with wavy dark hair came into Desiree's mind. He'd been on the high school football team, his broad chest and strong shoulders emphasized by his well-fitting jersey. He'd been a couple of years ahead of her, and had never given her a passing glance.

She'd glimpsed him at the homecoming game—the only one she and Candee had ever attended. When you lived in as many foster homes as they had, high school socializing was non-existent. Someone had pointed him out as the wealthiest kid in town. From what Desiree had heard, he sometimes helped his parents with their pub, key word being *sometimes*. Usually he was too busy escorting the current prom queen to country club dances, or driving around in his shiny new Ferrari after football practice.

After the game, she'd thought about talking with him, because her heart skipped a beat as she'd watched him. But, he'd been too engrossed in flirting shamelessly with a pretty cheerleader to notice Desiree.

Talk about a guy being off limits. In any event, they had run in completely different social circles. That is, if living in foster care counted as a circle.

"Teddy believes you can benefit from Keiran's carpentry skills," Candee said.

Panic rose inside Desiree. There would be a huge amount of work involved in transforming this house into her dream, and she remembered Keiran as seeming to be the opposite of ambitious.

Was it too late to sell her house back to Teddy and admit she'd made a mistake?

She pressed back her panic and concentrated on the second-story porch—the bracketed columns and neglected ornamental detail.

And the two words the house screamed: money pit.

She grimaced. "How does Teddy know Keiran?" she asked.

"Keiran remodeled a kitchen and bath in Georgia and someone from Teddy's crew saw his work and recommended him."

Another gust of wind made the women shiver, and Candee jammed one hand into the pocket of her gray hoodie. "Earlier today, Teddy called Keiran and hired him for your project."

Desiree scowled. "Your husband did all this without asking me first?

"The guy's cheap, remember? He's coming back to his hometown and you'll be his—"

Desiree hesitated to finish the sentence. And then she did. "His first client."

"Exactly." Candee cheerfully ignored Desiree's apprehensive glance. "You want to host Christmas Eve dinner in your new house, correct? You can't do that until your kitchen is in working order."

"Regardless, I've never been known for my culinary skills. Except for my pistachio cake."

Candee laughed. "Um, even that's debatable."

The giggles came easier now, and Desiree's mind raced

with trying to find a good reason to refuse Keiran's help before he arrived.

"I'd like to see his work. I have a certain design in mind, shabby chic, and I want it to be flawless," she said.

The laughter faded from Candee's face. "Flawlessness isn't the only thing that matters. Sometimes you take what you can get depending on your budget." She extracted Desiree's house key from her purse.

So that was where the key had gone. Desiree had forgotten she'd given it to Candee for safekeeping. Was this a sign she didn't really want the house?

Don't be ridiculous. If it was a sign of anything, it was that she was absentminded.

Candee lifted the key in the air. "Be content."

"Contentment and flawless should always be part of the same sentence."

"Not in our home-flipping world." Candee did a slow whirl, motioning toward the majestic trees, the worn picket fence, the trampled, overgrown bushes. A recent rain had soaked the lawn, and the grass was smeared with clumps of wet clippings. "Every house is a challenge and yours is no exception." She caught Desiree's hand. "C'mon. We've prolonged the inevitable long enough."

Sharing a chuckle, the women stepped onto the porch. Candee inserted the key into the lock, clicked the brass handle, and held the door open. "After you."

They stepped across a straw welcome mat, leaving footprints in the layer of dust on the aged parquet floor. Candee switched on the lights and offered a bright smile. "Oh, and there's one more thing about Keiran."

Desiree hesitated. "Only tell me if it's good."

"He planned on renting a place in town until he got on his feet," Candee said. "So Teddy recommended your attic apartment. He assumed you wouldn't mind if Keiran lived there for a while. The rent payment will help you with the mortgage."

A light fixture in the hallway swung precariously from an unsightly wire, and Desiree silently grumbled. "Is Keiran also an electrician?"

"Possibly, but he may not be licensed. I'm sure Teddy will know someone who is, though."

"Will a free room equal free labor?" Desiree waved off her sister's assurances. "And will his results be immediate? I want the house presentable by Christmas."

"C'mon, Desiree, don't be impatient. You're obliged to supply him with a salary and money for materials. Celebrate your good fortune because he dropped directly into your lap." Candee checked her watch. "Joseph's school bus will be coming soon. The school has early release because of a teacher planning seminar. I'll text you later."

With a nod signaling agreement, Desiree accepted the muffins and thanked her sister.

She took two paces into the foyer. A bone-deep weariness made her anxious, whereas Candee's enthusiasm was a source of inspiration.

Desiree drew on that inspiration. Taking a deep breath, she marched through the foyer and headed to the living room. The stained gold carpeting was peeling at the edges, and she bent to fold it back. Beneath the carpet were hardwood floors crying out for refinishing.

A large marble fireplace took up half the wall, its wide mantel solid oak. At Christmas, she imagined the mantel transformed, complete with sprigs of holly, miniature tealights and classic quilted stockings.

An unexpected downpour spilled across the bay window, and Desiree hoped that Candee had beaten the rain and reached her house without getting soaked.

She passed her fingers over the mantel, locating several

candles and a box of matches, a reminder that Teddy had used the fireplace. He'd mentioned the HVAC unit wasn't operating, which meant no central heating or air conditioning.

The lights in the foyer blinked, then went out.

Already? Desiree massaged her temples. She hadn't been in her new home ten minutes.

Have faith, and everything will fall into place. Practical matters first. The encouraging words from her "forever family" foster mother came to mind.

Certainly, Desiree thought, she should hold fast to that wisdom.

First, deal with the electrical problem. And then the plumbing, then the . . .

The list went on and on.

Whereas now she had Keiran, the playboy turned carpenter who was on some kind of bizarre mission to help the community.

She went to the kitchen and placed the muffin box on the counter. Quickly, she captured her tote bag carrying overnight necessities, climbed the oak staircase to the master bedroom, and changed into an old pair of jeans and a flannel shirt. Although the light would soon fade, she'd begin the first afternoon in her new house by scrubbing the tiled floor.

Fun way to spend a Monday evening, she thought wryly. Fortunately, the plumbing was functional, and Teddy had kept a pail of cleaning supplies beneath the sink.

Although she had a love/hate relationship with scrubbing floors, she rolled up her sleeves and eased into a pair of rubber gloves to protect her hands. She loved the way the floors gleamed after a thorough cleaning, and the fresh lemony smell, barring the exhausting, manual labor that went with it.

Either way, she'd prayed over her decision to purchase the

house, and with prayer came peace of mind. So she could do this. And she'd accept Keiran's help, because the financial savings would be tremendous.

That is, as long as he cut her a good deal, stayed in his attic apartment, and they maintained a working relationship.

And if he wasn't happy about that arrangement, he could book a hotel in town.

End of Chapter One

1-800-CHRISTMAS, the second book in the 1-800-Series by Josie Riviera ***

Copyright © 2018 Josie Riviera

Want more? Keep reading 1-800-CHRISTMAS.

The full 1-800-Series is available here.

ABOUT THE AUTHOR

Josie Riviera is a *USA TODAY* bestselling author of contemporary, inspirational, and historical sweet romances that read like Hallmark movies. She lives in the Charlotte, NC, area with her wonderfully supportive husband. They share their home with an adorable shih tzu, who constantly needs grooming, and live in an old house forever needing renovations.

Become a member of my Read and Review VIP Facebook group for exclusive giveaways and ARCs.

To connect with Josie, visit her webpage and subscribe to her newsletter. As a thank-you, she'll send you a free sweet romance novella directly to your inbox.

josieriviera.com

PRAISE AND AWARDS

USA TODAY bestselling author

#1 Amazon Bestseller Holiday Fiction

**#1 Amazon Bestseller Romance Collections &
Anthologies**

#9 Amazon Bestseller Contemporary Romance

ACKNOWLEDGMENTS

An appreciative thank you to my patient husband, Dave, and our three wonderful children.

ALSO BY JOSIE RIVIERA

Seeking Patience

Seeking Catherine (always Free!)

Seeking Fortune

Seeking Charity

Seeking Rachel

The Seeking Series

Oh Danny Boy

I Love You More

A Snowy White Christmas

A Portuguese Christmas

Holiday Hearts Book Bundle Volume One

Holiday Hearts Book Bundle Volume Two

Holiday Hearts Book Bundle Volume Three

Holiday Hearts Book Bundle Volume Four

Holiday Hearts Book Bundle Volume Five

Candleglow and Mistletoe

Maeve (Perfect Match)

A Love Song To Cherish

A Christmas To Cherish

A Valentine To Cherish

A Christmas Puppy To Cherish

A Homecoming To Cherish

A Summer To Cherish

Romance Stories To Cherish

Romance Stories To Cherish Volume Two

Cherished Hearts Six Book Volume

Aloha To Love

Sweet Peppermint Kisses

Valentine Hearts Boxed Set

1-800-CUPID

1-800-CHRISTMAS

1-800-IRELAND

1-800-SUMMER

1-800-NEW YEAR

The 1-800-Series Sweet Contemporary Romance Bundle

Irish Hearts Sweet Romance Bundle

Holly's Gift

A Chocolate-Box Christmas

A Chocolate-Box New Years

A Chocolate-Box Valentine

A Chocolate-Box Summer Breeze

A Chocolate-Box Christmas Wish

A Chocolate-Box Irish Wedding

Chocolate-Box Hearts

Chocolate-Box Hearts Volume Two

Chocolate-Box Double Hearts

Recipes From The Heart

Leading Hearts

New Year Hearts

SENIOR HEARTS

Summer Hearts

Christmas in the Air (1-800-Book)

A Very Christian Christmas

The 1-800-Series Volume Two

The 1-800-Series Complete

Christmas Tails of the Heart

Cocoa's Christmas Love

Pawfect Christmas Hearts

Pink Coral Island

Whispers of Love in Sweetwater Springs

Whispers of Maple Memories in Sweetwater Springs

Whispers of Holiday Magic in Sweetwater Springs

Whispers of Sweetwater Springs

A Harvest of Miracles

A Winter Promise

A Season Out of Time

Hearts and Horseshoes

1-800-CUPIDON (French Edition)

1-800-CUPDO (Spanish Edition)

1-800-AMOR (German Edition)

Most books are available in ebook, audiobook, paperback, Large Print paperback and Hardcover.

Many are FREE on Kindle Unlimited!

A GIFT FOR YOU

To keep up on newly released ebooks, paperbacks, Large Print Paperbacks, audiobooks, as well as exclusive sales, I invite you to sign up for Josie's Newsletter today.

As a thank you, I'll send you a free PDF: The Beauty Of

Josie's Newsletter

Did you know that according to a Yale University study, people who read books live longer?

.